BOLT FROM THE BLUE

Jeremy Cooper is a writer and art historian, author of five previous novels and several works of non-fiction, including the standard work on nineteenth century furniture, studies of young British artists in the 1990s, and, in 2019, the British Museum's catalogue of artists' postcards. Early on he appeared in the first twenty-four of BBC's *Antiques Roadshow* and, in 2018, won the first Fitzcarraldo Editions Novel Prize for *Ash before Oak*.

'*Bolt from the Blue* is a scintillating, wistful exploration of a good career and a poor relationship. Pithy yet expansive, it's an essential, engrossing, illuminating read for any aspiring artist.'
— Sara Baume, author of *handiwork*

'There's a strange magic to Jeremy Cooper's writing. The way he puts words together creates an incantatory effect. Reading him is to be spellbound, then. I have no idea how he does it, only that I am seduced.'
— Ben Myers, author of *The Offing*

'For a book that has the word 'love' on almost every page, *Bolt from the Blue* is endlessly inventive in showing us how love is often hidden, rationed, coded and disguised. It is an epistolary dialogue between a life of possibilities – as shown through the maturing vision of an artist – and one of disappointments, expressed through the wise and seasoned scepticism of the artist's mother. Jeremy Cooper is a deft and sensitive writer who understands how to entrust his book to his characters.'
— Ronan Hession, author of *Leonard and Hungry Paul*

'A novel written in epistolary form, Cooper has maximised the potential of this literary convention to achieve a work of great depth and quiet power. ... At times spellbinding and mesmerising, the work also proves provocative and inspirational. As much a love letter to the lost art of letter-writing as it is a thirty year-long dialogue of familial love, Cooper has produced an understated book that nonetheless resonates powerfully. This book is deeply sensitive to the ebb and flow of relationships over time and the way love is disguised, expressed and experienced, and it achieves that elusive dream of all authors and finds new meaning in the recording of life.'
— Helen Cullen, *Irish Times*

Fitzcarraldo Editions

BOLT FROM THE BLUE

JEREMY COOPER

To Lindsay Seers and Ben Rivers

To keep things straightforward and, as far possible, honest, I have precisely transcribed all the postcards and letters, later emails, I could find between my mother and me from my moving down to London in October 1985 until her death in August 2018. It turns out that we each kept a fair number through thirty years of moves and marriages. Mum's letters to me I had stacked in date order in an empty drawing-paper box in my studio, inside their envelopes, the emails in a folder of consecutive printouts. My letters to her I found in a jumble at the back of a clothes drawer, emails on her low-tech old PC in a file titled GIRL. The arrival of the internet and email does not appear to have much affected the way Mum and I wrote to each other. My last words to her were on a postcard. We were hooked by then into set habits of language and form. Subjects changed with time, as did the relationship, the basic structure of our connection hardly at all.

My letters and postcards and emails were always dated, hers never. Not all the time-gaps are due to missing letters, as one or other of us, usually both, regularly went silent. I can also see that some absences of information in the letters may be due to the intervention of our very occasional telephone calls. This does not explain all the empty months, nor the way some letters refer to the contents of another letter which no longer exists. Dozens of letters were allowed to disappear. There may be an explicit reason why, for example, the year 1987 is almost a complete letter-blank, together with the first half of 1988, but it is too long ago for me to meaningfully recall the circumstances. Several significant occurrences to fill various gaps over the years do spring arbitrarily to mind, in visual detail, without my knowing why there are no letters recording the event. In more recent years I was frequently away, researching and making my films, then showing them, often abroad, too preoccupied to write and uncontactable by Mum.

While I can remember a few of the letters from me that Mum did not keep, most of the absences are lost in the mist. I prefer to leave them there, in limbo. My policy is to look forward not back. Cut off and move on. My motto.

Some of Mum's letters which I do not have I tore up and threw away within seconds of reading them, they made me so angry. Others have simply vanished, maybe left by me in a jacket pocket and discarded by the dry cleaners, or abandoned by mistake on a café table. Neither of us were great letter-writers anyway. Even if I had them all, the narrative they tell would still be partial. Nothing is ever complete, everything always a version. An illusion to imagine that diligent research and enquiry, about anything or anyone, can produce the whole story. There is no such thing.

This is what I have.

Period.

Patterns coalesce, sometimes by chance, at other times by design.

It took years, but our contact did seem to find, in time, a worthwhile rhythm, tightness and tedium giving way to a skewed sense of connection and care.

The letters tell only a tiny part of what has happened to me as an adult. They offer even fewer details of Mum's life.

Re-reading this correspondence was a disturbing experience.

I cannot deny that these are my words and yet they do not feel like me. A depleted with-mother me? Although flashes of my actual presence are seen in a fair number of thoughts which I still hold today, this remains a selective misrepresentation of who I am. The temptation to add and improve, to remove repetition, tone down my rants, was considerable.

I am pleased that I managed to resist. Because inconsistency, contradiction and exaggeration I have come to accept as the marks of reality, proof that, however inadequate in terms of communication and inaccurate as history, these letters are right. True, in my seeing, gathered by me for myself alone and not for others.

It is difficult, I find, to match the Lynn Gallagher who wrote these letters to the person who made the films described, even though I am both these women.

I made the transcriptions over several months, bit by bit, in an effort to establish to my own satisfaction why the outwardly unexceptional relationship between a mother and daughter affected me badly for so many years. The effort was wasted. Work on the texts has told me nothing. To the present me, my past feelings remain in essence inexplicable. Rereading these pages, I cannot understand how Mum's behaviour drove me to physically cut myself away from whatever it was in her that I felt the need to protect myself from.

Where in these letters is there evidence of maternal ill-treatment?

That is what I have been asking myself, and am obliged to answer 'Nowhere'. In between a line or two, or ten, maybe.

Nothing serious.

Would I have written so many letters with 'news and views' if our relationship was as bad as I constantly told myself it was? Equally, it is unlikely that I would recently have spent masses of time on this project of reclamation had it not felt important for me to do so.

While I do care that my films and photographs are seen – art-things do not exist until entering the lives of others – this does not alter the fact that the work matters essentially to me, will forever matter most to me, whatever anybody else might feel about it. Even more so with the transcript of these letters, my making of a private memento to Mum and me.

It is true what Mum used to say, that at heart I have never much cared what others think, preoccupied instead with my own concerns.

In my mid-fifties now, I have led a rich life, to which Mum appears in these letters to have contributed more than she took away. Her self-negating acceptance of things may have tied Mum down but it did not hold me back. The mistakes I made are my own and it is ridiculous of me to blame her, as I have tended to do for far too long.

We suffer. Of course we suffer, from time to time. Some people a great deal more than others. I have been lucky.

Sadly, alongside my narrow-minded account of art things, this correspondence mostly tells of our family difficulties. All the same, I hope some real qualities in Mum's and my relationship manage to push their way through.

These letters are letters, not literature.

I am a maker of films not a writer, and Mum was neither.

One thing which surprises me is the overlapping language, the shared phrases, related tone. Probably because it is me to her and her to me, us to each other. I write differently to my friends, and to myself.

My thoughts at least are not my mother's.

I don't think they are.

Are they?
Don't tell me, I'd rather not know.

1 OCT 85

Mum

Busy, brief.

Arrived safely and found the college digs easily enough.

Direct by 19 bus to St Martin's.

St Martin's College of Art! How about that!!

I feel ... I feel happy.

Love

Lynn xx

7 OCT 85

Mum

Me again.

It's great here: London, the school, the students.

I feel at home. It's where I'm meant to be.

Already into a routine. You know how I need routine. For the first few days I couldn't find any time to read my novel-of-the-moment, which worried me. Now, if nothing else, I've at least thirty-five minutes twice a day on the top deck of the bus to and from St Martin's. To bury myself in a story.

Decided to tackle Doris Lessing.

Not 'tackle', that makes it sound a chore. It's not. Not at all. She's wonderful. I meant that I intend to read several, beginning at her first, *The Grass is Singing*, then move straight on to *The Golden Notebook*, which is the one I'm most looking forward to. Finishing off with *The Good Terrorist*, just out in paperback.

With the scholarship, I'm able to buy every book I read – second-hand if necessary – and will begin to make my own grown-up library.

Most of the teachers are practising artists and understand

that the point is to encourage and support, not tell.
Midwives not policemen.
So refreshing after the drag of eleven-plus and O-levels and A-levels, and the portfolio and interviews for here. No more exams, ever! It's all coursework, and assessment of stuff made. Not a problem.
I think so, anyway.
Must rush.
Love
Lynn

17 OCT 85

Mum
Have you got the correct address? Lynn Gallagher (First Year), St Martin's College of Art, 107-109 Charing Cross Road, London WC2H 0EB. Each student has her own pigeonhole, where event notices and timetables and letters are placed twice a day. Except I haven't received a single letter.
Nothing to tell you. I'm not going to write into thin air.
Lynn x

28 OCT 85

Mother
Take a jump.
Lynn

[Written in black ink capital letters on the message side of a Leeds Postcard, the front with a field of grey pound signs overlaid in block lettering with the slogan: *I DON'T GIVE A SHIT WHAT YOUR HOUSE IS WORTH.*]

Dear Lynn

Sorry, love, haven't been feeling too good. Taken on more shifts at the pub, now that you're not here in the evenings. It'll sort itself out.
Glad to hear you're settling in.
You're my star.
Lots of love
Mum

P.S. Great card. Money, that's all anyone thinks about, isn't it?

3 NOV 85

Dear Mum
We're making postcards at St Martin's.
B-NEGATIVE painted in my own dark red blood! Not a cow's!
My tutor liked it a lot. Now it's yours.
Love
L x

[Posted the postcard in an envelope, to prevent damage. Strange now to handle something I made over thirty years ago and had not seen again until clearing Mum's flat. Like most of my past work, I remembered precisely how it looked.]

—

Dear Lynn
Dead right title for you!

Wasn't it hysterical when the school nurse told us you were this rare blood type? They were always calling you to give blood. Useful earner.
I've settled in.
To my new hours at The Blind Traveller.
And to controlling the booze.
Ankles swollen from the extra-standing. Better than they were. You get used to anything, in the end.
See you.
Love
Mum

19 NOV 85

M
Beware of apples'n'onions bunions!
How's Chippy puss?
Does she miss me?
I miss her!
L xx

[Embarrassing Kardorama postcard of a fluffy grey kitten playing with a large ball of yellow wool.]

18 DEC 85

Mum
I'm afraid I won't be home for Christmas or New Year.
A friend has invited me to stay at her parents' place, near Exeter. Sounds like quite a large house.
She's got a car, so we'll be driving down
Her father runs the family firm of stockbrokers. Four days a week in the City. That kind of stuff.

As it's your busy time at the pub you'll barely notice.
Love
Lynn

20 JAN 86

Mum
How are you? Was Christmas OK?
I've caught a cold, touch of flu perhaps. Never mind, it'll pass.
Full of ideas for work
Lynn xx

[Written on the classic Guerrilla Girls postcard of a billboard in New York showing the Mona Lisa with a green gag, the black and pink capital letters reading: *First they want to take away a woman's right to choose. Now they're censoring art.*]

—

Dear Lynn
Xmas was fine, thanks. Plenty of visitors, people dropping by. At the pub, mostly,
Bought myself a new radio in the sales. And fancy underwear. Yeah, I'm in pretty good shape. Considering.
Didn't have to do Christmas turkey or anything. Don't know why I bothered all those years.
Love
Mother

P.S. The cat's fine too. No cat has ever missed anybody. Nor any other cat, as far as I can see. Food and warmth all they go for.

Mum

Thought it was Christmas at home which I find impossible. Bliss compared with Devon!

Safest, I'd say, to pretend the visit never happened. Except I've been trying to blank it out, and can't. So, need to get it off my chest. To you, of course!

One of my lists!

That fucking family. Frisky, freezing, freaky, fraudulent, frantic, foxy, foul, fossilised, formal, forlorn, footling, foolish, foetid, fly-blown, fleshy, flatulent, flash, flaky, filthy, fiendish, fidgety, feeble, faulty, fat, fatal, farcical, false.

Reverse alfabetical!

Jerk of a father made a pass at me.

They have an outdoor swimming pool. Heated, in winter!

On the way out, this breed. They must be. Surely?

I'm going to ignore Christmas completely from now on.

Love

Lynn

Dear Mum

There's a teacher at St Martin's who bangs on about contact-making, how important it is for our careers. Weird! Since when did being an artist become a career?

If it is then I don't want to be an artist. I do stuff, that's all. Stuff which may or may not mean anything to anybody else. To me, though, it really matters. That's the point.

Love

Lynn

P.S. St Martin's College of Art is now officially called the London Institute. Makes no difference.

28 FEB 86

Mum

You asked if I had somewhere to work at college.

I do, it's great: open long hours, seven days a week. First year students have individual studios on the lower ground floor. Cubicles, with eight-foot high wooden divides, open on the passage side, no doors.

Looking out of the window, below the level of the pavement, I can see passers-by up to the top of their thighs.

Fascinating. I could watch for hours. Who are they? Where've they come from, where are they going to? I'm obsessed!

'Tell me another,' I hear you saying!

Out of the hundreds and hundreds of Polaroids I've taken, I've selected a hundred and thirty and mounted them flush-floated in a Perspex box frame, ten across by thirty down. Made the whole thing myself.

Spent days fiddling with patterns, direction of travel, coat colours, male/female, etc. One dog, placed near the bottom right of my grid, pissing against the railings. Can't see his willy.

My photographic grid echoes the old iron bars on the window. Sort of.

Enclosed is a Polaroid of the Polaroids.

What do you reckon?

Love

L xx

—

Dear Lynn
I like it when you ask my opinion.
What do I think of your ... what would you call it? A picture?
Don't think much of it, to be honest. Looks a bit of a mess.
You've always been so very tidy, and organised. I hope they don't
ruin that for you at art school.
See how it goes. Keep K V.
Love
Mother

26 JUNE 86

Mum

Last night I had an experience I'll never forget. Ever.

At the Almeida Music Festival I saw John Cage, the man himself, face of wrinkles and smiles. Plus his fat fellow-American pianist with a droopy moustache. In a performance of *4'33"*.

Do you know about this piece?

Cage wrote it soon after the war.

Mikhashoff, the pianist, sat down at the grand piano, closed the lid, set a stopwatch, folded his hands in his lap and rested in solemn and silent concentration for precisely four minutes and thirty-three seconds. After which he turned off the watch, opened the lid to expose the keys, stood up and bowed. To rapturous applause from the audience and a hug from Cage.

Creaks of the floor, a man in the third row clearing his throat, cups clinking in the café outside. Loads of music! The near-silent sound of my own breath, blood beating in my ears.

I've never seen anything like it. I mean, there's no-one like Cage, or his music, and I've never seen or heard either live before. Of course not. I'm twenty-one and until nine months ago I'd hardly moved from a Birmingham suburb!

Despite his size, Yvar Mikhashoff is a champion tango dancer, it said in the programme. Not his real name, an art self-christening. Pinched from his grandfather, who, he claims, was a Russian general.

London!

London!!

London!!!

Love from Lynn

29 JUNE 86

Mum

I told you money's short and I'll need to work through the summer?

Would've been at home, the usual, Sparkhill Co-op, if I hadn't landed this great job up in Newcastle. At the Hatton Gallery, attached to the university. Tom, my tutor, knows the head of art there and recommended me for freelance work – cataloguing a collection of British drawings they've just been given. I'm thrilled.

I'll let you know how it goes.

Take care of yourself.

Make sure lover-boy does his share in the house.

Big wish!

Love

Lynn

—

Lynn

Are you never ever coming home again in your whole life?

Mother

[I remember at the time wondering what the connection was between the image on this postcard and her words. None the wiser today. Maybe it was a card Mum happened to have lying around, perhaps one I left behind in my room? It is captioned *What price defence?* by the photomontage specialist Peter Kennard, of a billion-pound note passed into a skeletal hand in exchange for missiles. On the reverse is a quotation from 1980 by Francis Pym, Defence Secretary at the time: *We have to possess the most horrific weapons precisely so as not to use them.*]

28 SEPT 86

Mum
Back in London getting ready for term.
It was brilliant up North, exactly the type of work I like. After sorting the drawings into some kind of order, I devised an effective method of categorization and piled through them.
The experience of looking hard, for weeks on end, at other people's art-ideas. At drawings, at the heart of things, hand to pencil to paper. Leaves me with a respect for the act of making miles beyond my previous thoughtlessness. Making things is a serious business. No fooling.
Lynn xxx

4 OCT 86

Mum
A thought.
The thing which excites me about looking at non-commercial exhibitions, at the Whitechapel, say, or the Serpentine, is feeling the vitality in the best of these

older artists. A sense of their energy of endeavour, in everything they did, a lasting presence in their work after the death of the body.

Love

Lynn xx

[Sent this on a words-only postcard: *MAKE LOVE NOT BABIES – BAN THE POPULATION BOMB.*]

—

Dear Lynn

Wanted to tell you how pleased I am you're finding your way forward.

Pleased for you, not myself.

True.

I had my chances and didn't take them. You have. Good for you, luv.

Forget that nonsense about daughters fulfilling their mothers' dreams. Flipping insult. To us both.

Make your own bed, I say, and sleep on it yourself. No room for me. Wouldn't want to anyway. Jesus, you shared my bed for long enough when you were little!

As it happens, I agree with you about getting a kick up the pants from looking at tip-top art. I mean, that Picasso, he can do anything. Always making stuff nobody'd dreamt of doing before. Can't stand half of it myself. So what?

I love his hands, in the photos.

Keep it up! Strength to strength!

With love

Mother

—

Dear Lynn
I can't believe you're AGAIN not coming up for Christmas.
I don't understand. You say refusing to see me isn't personal.
Bloody well feels like it, I can tell you!
Barely remember what you look like. Never saw much of you
anyway. Out at school, or staying-over with friends.
Suppose you cut off all your lovely hair once I wasn't around
to stop you?
Never mind. It's your life. I don't mind.
All I want is to see you home for Christmas.
Love
Mother

14 DEC 86

Mum
I never said I refused to see you, just that I don't want to
step foot in Sparkhill. Not for the time being, anyway.
Not necessarily forever.
I've told you why. If you don't get it, that's not my fault.
There's nothing stopping you from coming to see me!
Do you? No.
Do you ever even suggest it? No.
Please, don't make such a fuss. I know it's not normal.
Nothing is 'normal'. Not with us or anybody else.
This is how we meet, in letters and postcards. For now.
We're getting on fine.
Don't rock the boat you used to tell me, when I took
against your boyfriends.
Same to you now. Different circumstances, same prin-
ciple.
Let go, please.
Love
Lynn

Mum

All the talk at London art schools this summer is about *Freeze*.

Pretty annoying, as nobody seemed to notice our degree show. Doesn't really matter. I was happy enough with my drawings. Which won a prize, actually!

Don't imagine news of *Freeze* reached Sparkhill!

It's a show of their own work organised by final year students at Goldsmiths, in a disused gym down Deptford way.

Don't wait to be asked, we'll do it for ourselves!

A short ballsy bloke from Leeds is the ringleader. He's a whirlwind. Persuaded the developers across the river in Canary Wharf to pay for publication of an A4 illustrated catalogue. For a bunch of students!

I liked Gallaccio's piece best, the colours and shapes made by pouring molten lead over the floor. Apparently, she burnt her foot in an early session and couldn't walk, her colleagues rallying round to finish the work for her, while she sat at the side giving instructions. 'We were all Anya's slaves,' one of the other students said. 'While she hung about on crutches drinking a glass of wine!'

They were their own curators, taking turns to open up and sell catalogues. While I was there two of the small coloured cardboard boxes in Hirst's sculpture fell off the wall and Fairhurst, I think it was, stuck them back in place.

Derivative stuff, self-deciding to abandon ship. He's the Leeds lad. A way to go.

Pretty inspiring, though, all in all.

Or is it a storm in a teacup?

I wonder.

Telling you about it helps me see things from the outside. Cuts the London art dragon down to size.
Love
Lynn

3 FEB 89

Mum
Relieved to say that I've got a part-time job. My friend Georgie, from the year above, found it for me. Studio assistant to a painter called Cedric Dawson. Big decorative rubbish. Him too. Fat, all flowery shirts and innuendo. Suits me perfectly. Go in, do my job without a thought, pocket the cash and get on with my own thing.
It's friends I talk to. Like Georgie. Not past-it pricks.
She told me that once when the Director did his studio rounds with them last year, he looked into one cubicle, then outside in the passage was heard to complain, shaking his head: 'There's one in every year.'
Bloody rude!
Must ask Georgie whose studio it was. Probably turn out to be a star!
Must rush.
Love
L xx

27 FEB 89

Mum
Can't believe what I heard last night on the radio.
President Reagan defends his fitness for office by the fact that he can still put on his socks without sitting down!
Lynn xx

[On a postcard of Margaret Thatcher with her head in her hands above the red-edged banner: *Maggie Shock. American Failure To Buy Britain.*]

—

L
I've stopped myself asking you this dozens of times, but ... Do you have a boyfriend? Or girlfriend, I don't mind. Is there any-one you love?
M xx

[Written on a commercial postcard view of the National Exhibition Centre in Birmingham, the same side of town as Sparkhill, not far from home.]

20 MAR 90

Mum, you're so funny! I knew this was the one thing you really wanted to know!
No, I don't.
I did.
Off and on.
A very clever artist and utter arsehole. Unbelievably self-centred. I suppose I thought I could change him. Standard woman stuff.
He was at the Slade. I saw the light in the end and floored him by saying that I felt lonelier with him than on my own!
Tant pis, as they say.
Not that I'm certain I know what that means
Tant pis, all the same.
xLx

Mum

If you want me to tell you about boyfriends, you're also going to have to listen to me bang on about art. Though both subjects frequently bore me rigid!

Pleased to have come across an artist, a couple of years older than me, whose work I like a lot. Michael Landy. His dad's Irish. A show he calls *Market* has just opened in Bermondsey and I went earlier today.

Takes on an enormous space, a decommissioned biscuit factory, set out with piles of coloured plastic crates and ranks of metal market stalls covered in rolls of fake grass. Empty. No fruit or veg. Nothing.

Wandering around there on my own I felt even more self-conscious than I usually do at exhibitions. Not sure why. Relieved to be drawn towards the sounds of a video piece he's made, in a room at the side.

'No choice ... That's it, simple, there's no choice. From quite early on, already at secondary school ... I mean, and then, after art school, you just drive forward, whatever the setbacks,' Landy says.

I agree.

Love

Lynn

4 JAN 91

Mum

I give up.

Love!!

Me, I thrash around in perpetual misunderstanding. Love may seem on occasion to work. It never does, though. Never can, I reckon. Doomed.

No use asking you to elucidate!
LOVE from me xx

[Written on another Leeds Postcard, Angela Martin's stylised watercolour of a disgruntled woman, titled *Famous Radical Feminist Sayings* and captioned *Dead as a Dildo.*]

—

Dear Lynn
What do you mean?
Don't be so rude.
May not be the standard deal but I've had a lot of love in life. Given plenty, that's for sure. Happy to have. Love's not a balance sheet, you know. It doesn't cost anything. Giving love to someone is gain not loss.
What's more, it's you who can't understand, won't listen. Not me who can't explain.
You don't actually want to know, if truth be told.
Love
Mother

6 MAR 91

Mum
At the end of last year I jacked in my job with that lousy Cedric Dawson.
Mustn't do this again. Anything's better than working for a crappy artist. Hat-check girl. I don't mind. Pole-dancer? Maybe not. Too thin, minimal boobs.
Don't have to, anyway. Susan Hiller has asked me to help with her Freud Museum project, and she's the tops, in my view.

At Matt's Gallery last year, I spent ages looking at her film installation, with those boxing skeletons. Badgered them to put me in touch with Hiller. I think she may have seen my work somewhere, or maybe Klassnik at Matt's had, I can't quite remember. Doesn't matter now.

Two days a week in her studio, a short walk from St John's Wood Underground, halfway to the Saatchi Gallery in Boundary Road.

I've loved being there from the first moment.

I'm lucky, I know.

Love

Lynn

P.S. Incidentally, Matt isn't a person. He's Robin Klassnik's large, very woolly English Sheepdog! The gallery also handles Joel Fisher and Mike Nelson, two other artists I like a lot.

20 MAR 91

Mum

Working for Susan Hiller is perfect. Instead of the loss of two days it's total gain.

1. She's intellectually inspiring.

2. I earn enough from her to cover my share of the flat's rent.

3. I get tons more done during the other five days than I ever did in seven.

The system is that Susan does the finding and fetching of the material for her Freud boxes, and writing the texts, while I do the setting and mounting in archive boxes.

She's very particular.

Which I like, as you know.

The first piece that I've finished is quite complex, with

cut-out slots to hold a wooden slapping stick and, bottom right, a magnifying glass focused on a Mr Punch postage stamp. In the lid, the photocopy of a photograph of a Punch & Judy performer talking to a boy from the audience.

She has titles for each box printed in capital letters on a rectangular white card stuck on the outside of the lid. This one's called: *SLAPSTICK (slaep' stik)*.

It's never dull with Susan. Earlier today, seeing my puzzled frown, she told me it's too late to question her sense of humour!

Indeed!

Why would I want to? She's such fun.

And democratic. Such a healthy vision of art. Considers viewers and listeners and readers to be active participants, as collaborators, interpreters, even detectives.

Go work it out, fellas!

With love

Lynn

—

Dear Lynn

Do you listen to the radio these days? You always used to.

I could never get what you saw in that Letter from America. *He always seemed to miss the point. Never trusted the man myself, his pretend innocence. Me, I ten times prefer the open crook to a closet deceiver. Worst are those who don't even know they're not telling the truth. Too far up their own arses to notice.*

Your weekly date with the Top Twenty *was all right, I must admit.*

Anyway, what I wanted to say is that Gardeners' Question Time *next week is from Solihull. I've got a ticket. And a question.*

What peach tree would the panel recommend I plant against the
sunny wall of a Sparkhill semi?
Trouble is I don't know what sort of soil it is. They're bound
to ask.
Don't suppose I'll get called. You might like to tune in, in case.
Love
Mother

2 MAY 91

Mother
Missed the programme, sorry.
Are you really going to plant a peach tree? You'll need
a team of your ex-blokes to pickaxe the concrete first!
I agree, plain-speakers much better than smarmy gits.
Doesn't politeness drive you mad? Does me. Bugger
manners. Society's thumb screws.
I keep changing my mind about the radio. There're days
when it feels productive to have Radio 4 playing in the
studio while I work. At other times I find any extra
sound a total distraction. Get so irritated by the small
mindedness of those middle-class, middle-aged, middle-
of-the-road, privately educated, politician-worshipping,
in-joke addicted, overpaid, time serving presenters.
And your years of *Archers*-worship at dinner send me
straight to the off-button the second that terrible tune
starts up.
I still listen a bit to Radio 3. Less than before, because
in London I can do my music-listening live. Mark up in
my diary dates in advance and book tickets.
Alone.
I love going to concerts of contemporary music on my
own. Listening and listening. And watching. Following
the conductor's hand to look for the sound about to be

made by the players.

The new music scene's so unaffected. No trendies, concert hall three-quarters full at the most, people there because they want to hear.

Not to see and be seen.

I never meet anybody who knows me. Another attraction.

With love

Lynn

23 MAY 91

Mum

A confession: I'm hooked on Boulez!

He's set up this experimental music school in Paris. Near the Pompidou, I think.

Anyhow, he brings his musicians over quite often to play at the Barbican.

I always go.

Took a note the other day of something he wrote: 'We must never give in and simply follow the existing rules, which are not difficult to observe ... but take action as direct as possible to transform those rules, which have often become nothing more nor less than the conventions of an established swindle.'

Phew!

Love

Lynn X

—

Dear Lynn
What's wrong with Mantovani, king of the strings?
A lot, I agree!

What I'd love to go to, one day, is the Bach B Minor Mass at
King's College. Your Aunt Betty's invited me a couple of times
but it's always been around Christmas, when I'm working.
On my visits to her in Cambridge we do go to the theatre. The
Footlights one year, with Hugh Laurie. I didn't laugh once.
Surprised she doesn't take me to concerts. Betty was always more
musical than me. Perhaps that's why. Afraid Mahler might be
beyond me!
The so-and-so!
Mother x

2 AUG 91

Mum

I made an exception last night to my no-previews rule,
for Sarah S., and went to the opening of the group show
she's in. *Broken English* at the Serpentine.

'Prestigious young British art', they're calling it.
Whiteread, Hirst, Landy and the rest.

She's laid out on the lawn in front of the gallery a massive
Union Jack of broken glass. Thousands and thousands
of smashed green and clear glass bottles. I spilt my glass
of wine laughing when Sarah said to me, RSC style: 'In
my mind, somewhere far away, in what was once called
British Empire, an ancient wind-ravaged Union Jack,
drained of all its colour, hangs abject, on a forgotten
flagpole.'

She's good!

It was difficult to take in the work, with the crowds and
chatter. And a touch too much to drink, to calm my
nerves.

Saw Sarah was wilting too. Persuaded her to leave early
and we walked arm-in-arm together down Exhibition
Road.

To Daquise, a cheap Polish restaurant near South Ken tube.
Where we talked in the kind of way I love.
Lynn XX

4 SEPT 91

Mum
This will infuriate you! More gossip about the tiny, tinny, trivial world of art!
This summer, a bloke called Gavin Turk, who failed his MA at the Royal College, has been taken on by White Cube as one of the five artists they've chosen to represent on opening in the West End. Stuff qualifications!
Hirst, of course, is one of the others.
Yeah, so what?
Right, seeing that White Cube is run by a rich name-grabber, the son of a Tory ex-minister, his gallery stands for everything people like me DO NOT want the art world to be.
Except Turk's different. I've never met him but I'm sure he is, you can tell from the work. Sure, he takes himself seriously. Never too seriously.
Enough!
Love
me xx

—

Dear Lynn
This Turk bloke sounds a bit like my dad, your grandfather, who you never met. Everyone liked him too.
I loved everything about him. His smile, his smell, his jokes. His oil-stained mechanic's hands. Sunday visits to the pub for lunch

with him and Mum, Betty and me included, he always insisted.
He drank, of course. Men drink. Though I never saw him out
for the count.
Died from blood poisoning, like plenty of blue-collar workers
in his day.
You're not like him at all. Or my mother.
And not remotely like your own useless dad.
Bolt from the blue, you!
M xx

21 NOV 91

Mum

I'm not being pathetic, not complaining. Just that I can only once remember you looking proper-happy when I was a girl.

Twice, to be precise, on the same day.

Preparing to go to and then returning from rehearsals for Handel's Messiah with Birmingham Amateur Choral Society. I reckon you must've loved singing. The unity of a choir, or something?

Maybe you had a beautiful voice and were proud of the sound you made?

Never showed an interest in other classical work, as far as I can remember.

How did you learn to read music? And Betty the piano, for that matter. Grandpa a mechanic.

It's possible, now I think of it, that you pretended to read the notes and sang by ear.

You've always been good at winging it!

Love

Lynn

17 DEC 91

Mum

You'll have noticed that I decided to save you from a blow-by-blow account of life in the Hiller studio. May not always be able to restrain myself!

So you know, though ... it's fantastic!

Love, Lynn

[Sent on a Cath Tate postcard from four or five years before, a photomontaged bottle of eye-bath treatment, the label with a wedding photo of the Prince and Princess of Wales, with the brand name Royal Eye Wash and printed at the base *Guaranteed Free of Homosexuality And Ethnic Minorities*.]

—

Lynn

What, there'll be MORE art news on the way?

You've already twice put me to sleep!

Seriously, you're writing like a robot. Or to a robot. In some letters I don't hear you or see myself.

Not much fun either way.

Ahoy there! It's me! The woman who used to do your cooking!

Mother x

10 FEB 92

Mum

You're not going to put me off! Aren't you a teeny bit interested in that shark in formaldehyde?

In our lunch break yesterday, Susan and I walked down to Boundary Road to see what the art-crowd are making such a fuss about.

Much as expected. Kind-of clever. Nose for publicity.

Enterprising of Hirst to pull it off technically and then flog the silly thing for a fortune to Charles 'the baron' Saatchi.

Susan has no time for art like this. She quite liked its title: *The Physical Impossibility of Death in the Mind of Someone Living*.

Must be a relief in Birmingham that the estate agent's been released unharmed. Eight days bound and gagged in a coffin in a padlocked workshop. No picnic.

The man, he'll be convicted.

I'll write again soon.

Love, Lynn

—

Dear Lynn

Stephanie Slater, yes, awful. She was lucky.

In the pub some know-all said the kidnapper, Sams, has only one leg.

Seems unlikely. You'd need to be nifty to catch an estate agent and shut her in a box, I reckon.

I can believe him being married three times. There's no accounting for the shitty men us idiots get tied up with.

Susan Hiller sounds a hoot.

xx Mum

16 SEPT 92

Mum

Who is it who comes up with the headlines?

Like 'Black Wednesday', 'The Great God ERM', 'Limp Lamont'.

I mean, limp rather than lame is genius!

I'm busy fixing boxes. Yesterday it was an ace Hiller number, with the photo of an American cowgirl called Jennie Metcalfe and two Staffordshire white china cow creamers.

Susan said she'd never heard women called cow until she came to England.

As she's a word buff, I should ask her about the origins of popular newspaper phrases. We've made a Freud archive box titled *NAMA-MA*, the word for mother in one of the Aboriginal dialects.

When she was in Australia not long ago, Papunya artists showed her where to find the earth pigments with which they make their paintings. She brought samples home, which I've ground and mounted in glass cosmetic containers, to place in a fitted compartment in the box.

Though she's a bit of a mystic, believes in auras and dreams and communication beyond the grave, Susan is super-conscious of the practicalities of making art. Very down to earth, essentially.

She's such a challenge!

Love, Lynn xx

—

Lynn

You haven't got the message, have you?

I tell you, I hate the way you lecture me about art. As if I'm a brick. A blank wall. 'Slap it on. Don't worry, she won't understand'.

Why bother, in that case?

As a matter of fact, I've always liked looking at paintings and sculpture and things, when I get the chance. Who do you think encouraged you in the first place?

Big field, can't see everything. You know what you know. Me, I happen to have heard of Hilliard and not Hiller, until you started in her studio. His work's pretty good too, don't you think? Saw his photographs a couple of years ago in the Barber Institute, over in Edgbaston, at the University.

You can be as critical of me as you like, just don't write me off as thick.

Bitch, if that's what you think. Not stupid bitch.

Mother

27 SEPT 92

Mum

Do I sound as though I don't give a toss what you think about my work?

It's complicated.

Sorry if that's how I come across. It'll probably be a hangover from when I was a teenager, convinced you weren't in the least bit interested in what I did. Sensed your desperation to get shot of me.

Both may be true. Or neither. I honestly don't know what I really feel.

About anything.

Except perhaps my work. Which for sure has a solid way to go yet.

Maybe I'll really want to know what you think when I've finally done something that I myself reckon might be worthwhile?

Time. It takes time. Everything takes such a very long time.

Be patient, please.

We'll get through.

With love

Lynn

7 OCT 92

Mum

I wake up early at the moment and can't get back to sleep. Lie there in the dark, thinking.

Several times recently about my childhood. Remembering how calm you were in a crisis. When I fell into a bank of nettles in the Norfolk dunes one baking summer's day and stung myself all over. On our holiday, in a caravan site.

Do you remember?

And me feeling sick in the coach on the way down to London, our first time on the M1, and you forcing the driver to stop on the hard shoulder and let me out for a breather.

All the sympathy and caring sent haywire by your angry eruptions at the drop of a hat.

Incidentally, I'm really pleased I speak with a Brummie twang. I usen't to be, when I first went to St Martin's. Got myself in a state about the dismissive assumptions by art-snobs. Which is everyone in the commercial art world, just about.

Seven years later I'm happy to hear the sounds I make. Pleased I didn't snuff them out in embarrassment.

With love

Lynn

25 JAN 93

Mum

Have you come across Morton's Dot-to-Dot postcards?

Lynn xx

[Sent her Paul Morton's postcard *Thatcher Therapy. Dot-*

to-Dot Puzzle No. 1, with instructions on the reverse: 'Thatcher Therapy. Take a broad, black, water-based felt-tip pen and follow the dots until Mrs Thatcher's face is obliterated. Wipe clean and it's ready for the next go. In no time at all you'll be looking forward to starting the day with fresh vigour.' Printed and published by Morton at his Hot Frog Graphics in Yorkshire.]

—

Dear Lynn
You chose that postcard on purpose, knowing how much I admire Mrs Thatcher!
Good laugh all the same.
She might be a bossy old bag but at least she speaks straight. I always know what she means. And quite often agree with her. Definitely about looking after the pennies. Family thrift, that kind of thing.
What about the threat to the climate, one of your sacred cows? Mrs Thatcher's right on side with that.
Doesn't fit so well with her work these days for Philip Morris, the tobacco people, I'll give you that!
I like getting your postcards. The postie winks at me when I answer the door on a postcard morning.
Love
Mum

P.S. Don't forget: I have NEVER voted Tory in my life, and never will.

18 MAR 93

Mum
'With due respect', 'if the truth be told', 'all things

considered', 'I have to say', 'frankly', and so on and so on. Whenever I hear phrases like this on the radio, I know I'm about to be lied to.

I've my suspicions even about the pseudo-innocent 'So ...'!

'To be honest...' implies, to me, that the remark about to follow is so marginally true as to be basically false! Every remark without this preface can presumably be taken as, at best, dubious? By intention or unknowingly. Makes little difference.

The other day a Tory MP claimed in a by-election programme on Radio 4: 'Chances are, if you vote for us England will win the World Cup and your daughter will marry a millionaire.'

Honestly!

No joke even if it is a joke.

I forgot to say a while back that, like your dad, Landy's dad was a working man. Built tunnels. Badly injured in the 1970s when a roof collapsed and has never been able to work since.

That's not funny either.

Love, Lynn

——

Don't be silly, love. Those clichés don't mean anything. They're just what everyone says. Without thinking.
M xx

[Mum wrote this on a Janet de Wagt postcard titled *Women are called birds because of the worms they pick up*, a drawing by the New Zealand artist who lived at the time in England, printed by the Tyneside Free Press Workshop.]

30 MAR 93

Mum
So it's great for everyone to go around saying what they don't mean? On the radio, in parliament, at school?
OK, I'll stop. Dead end!!
L xx

[Written on *Situationist Postcard No. 2* published by Exitstencil Press, designed by Gee Vaucher, female founder and lead singer of the anarcho-punk band Crass. A photomontage of a starving child served on a silver platter by a waiter to wealthy guests seated at a restaurant table.]

23 MAY 93

Mum
Things aren't easy, at the moment.
I've been selected for several group shows, and dealers are sniffing around. Reckoned I'd get by.
And I am, financially.
It's me. I'm the problem. My brain has collapsed. Into sponge. Moss.
Been reading the book *No Author Better Served*, of letters between Samuel Beckett and his American theatre director Alan Schneider, in one of which Beckett wrote: 'Not an idea in my head for new work of any kind – but then there never was.'
Ditto.
Double ditto, given the fact that when they did come Beckett's ideas were hundreds of times better than mine ever will be.

'Get a dog', you say. 'Have a baby'. I wish you'd stop making such ridiculous suggestions.

Please Mum.

Don't worry, I'll turn the corner.

With love

Lynn X

2 JUNE 93

Mum

Stroke of luck.

Not being in the swing, I hadn't heard about the studio-gallery set up by two young artists down Bethnal Green Road, close to Brick Lane. Until I happened to pick up – can't remember where, maybe at The Barley Mow – a copy of *Purple Prose*, with an article on them.

Walked straight over.

There they both were, sitting at a table making things.

I bought a white T-shirt with the hand-painted slogan in black capital letters HAVE YOU WANKED ON ME YET.

They're just doing what they do, not being 'artists'. It's great. In their *Purple Prose* interview one of the women said: 'We don't have a plan, we are the plan. I can't think of anything else I'd rather be doing.'

I'll keep an eye out for those two, that's for sure.

Love from Lynn

—

Dear Lynn

Sounds to me as if you're bang at the centre of things. No art-wanking in Birmingham!

Suppose they'll settle down soon enough to the standard slog.

46

Might as well enjoy themselves while they can.
Long live grants. And their dads probably slip them a fiver or
two now and again.
Is it all girls, or are there boy artists in the mix too?
Rather you than me.
With love
Mum

18 JUNE 93

Mum
Yeah, I think women are taking the lead these days, to some extent.
The men tend to be more conventional.
You're wrong about money from the dads, though, in this case. The father of one drives a taxi-cab and the other is married to a different woman from her mother!
When I was at the Brick Lane place three artist-friends of theirs dropped by. They were chatting about dealers and selling and stuff, and I overheard one of the two women say: 'I don't care how. All I want is to be rich and famous.'
'Give us a break, please,' one of the blokes responded, frowning in disbelief.
You never know. Determination gets you a long way.
I noted down from a Doris Lessing book: 'It's my belief that talent is plentiful, and that what is lacking is staying power.'
Off for a swim. Might try the London Fields Lido. Beautiful afternoon, and it's an outside pool.
Maybe it's no longer open? Saw something about it somewhere. Must check.
See you.
Love, Lynn

Mum

Susan's turning up with more and more things for me to box.

Yesterday it was a sandpainting she had picked up somewhere. Stylised teepee collage formed of different coloured sands 'collected from the deserts and mountains of the southwestern United States'. She's called it *PLIGHT (Plite)*, with an elaborate text pasted onto the inside of the lid.

I get the feeling Susan prefers to work alone, doing without studio assistants. She's warm and generous, but I tread carefully.

Don't blame her. I don't think I could ever co-direct a film. Need to do everything myself. Write the script, find locations, set the lights, hold the camera, edit the film, compose the credits.

Difficult enough managing the occasional actor, I find.

Would really like to do the acting too!

You run your own life, Mum. Maybe I caught the independence bug from you?

Dad seems to be a lazy, bloody ... What do I know? Haven't seen him since I was two and a half!

Let him go. Move on and let it go. That's what I must tell myself.

Love

Lynn

—

Dear Lynn

You mentioning your dad made me think of mine. As I often do. As you know.

It was he who arranged for my singing lessons, in Thetford, when I was sixteen. After the school told him I had a special voice.

He used to drive me over on a Sunday morning, his day off, and wait outside in the car, chain-smoking.

My teacher was blind.

I remember the dead leaves and litter blowing in the porch of her ground floor flat. No front step. And stumbling after her in darkness down a long passage when she answered the door.

Then her teaching room full of light, facing the yard. Which she couldn't see, of course.

The lessons were cut short by dad's death.

You're right, I never did learn to read music.

There's a lot I can't do.

Love

Mother

1 AUG 93

Dear Mum

That's sad about the singing. Without your dad I guess there'd have been no way for your mum to find the money to continue the lessons.

Coincidence that yesterday I went to something called the Fête Worse Than Death. I can see that for you there couldn't have been, at the time, a fate worse than your father's death. Must've affected everything

This FTWD was a street day-event put on by artists in Shoreditch. Planned now to be annual. The best bit about it was that almost all the participants, and the audience as well, knew each other. Us bystanders were involved in the act, our responses part of the show. Although there were maybe fifty stalls set out on both sides of the street, it was really intimate. Like a party at home.

49

Young artists performing with and for each other.

A few of my St Martin's lot were in the crowd. It was good to catch up.

Sarah S. and Georgie actually had stalls. With a bunch of the ex-Goldsmiths crew also doing their number. That Damien Hirst had a pitch. Stall set out with loads of tubes of paint, squares of cardboard and a turntable. His new thing: making spin paintings for a quid each. Hirst and Fairhurst, his studio-mate, were dressed and made-up as circus clowns, elaborately face-painted by big Leigh Bowery, the punk jeweller. For an extra 50p they exposed themselves, showed off their striped cocks and spotted balls!

Not for me, though. Too pally, in the end. A closed shop. Compston, the young man running it, has great energy but is quite a toff. Scent of swastika about the logo and retro line in waistcoats.

Got a good name for his outfit: Factual Nonsense.

Here's a typical FN slogan: 'So drop a flippin' stitch or two, pick up a piece and uplift your splendid soul.' Not bad, I have to admit!

Love

Lynn x

P.S. I'll try and mention names less. Doesn't matter who they are, whether publicly known or not. Will concentrate on what they do.

11 SEPT 93

Mum

I've been doing a lot of drawing. Comes out kind of weird but friends encourage me to go on with it.

This is one of the best, in my view.

50

What does it remind you of?
Love
Lynn

[This note and the folded drawing were still in the stiff brown envelope in which I had posted them.]

—

Dear Lynn,

Odd, as you say. Got something, though. I'm not qualified to say what it has but, as you asked my opinion, I'd say it looks skilful. I mean, it can't be easy to draw like that, realistic and sort of abstract at the same time.

Mind you, I can't see many people with your talent wanting to use it quite like this!

I'll ask your Aunt Betty what she sees in it.

Do you mind if I show Charmian too? I met her last year. She's a catering assistant at the National Exhibition Centre. We get on.

Won't take it to the pub, I promise!
Love
Mum

29 OCT 93

Mum

Tom, my old tutor at St Martin's, got in touch with a bunch of us to arrange to meet up at *House*, off Bow Road. It's a 'masterpiece', he says. Crap word. Fantastic artwork.

Difficult to describe. Won't try. You'll have to wait till there're photographs.

Even then you won't get the texture of the thing. Or feel

the threat of inside-outside, of wondering quite where you are.

I had to escape across the park to the canal and down the towpath for half a mile to stop myself going a bit crazy.

It was partly that I felt disappointed in myself, stabs of fear that I'm getting nowhere with my work. The artist is only two years older than me and she's done this monumental piece!

Think positively for me, please!

Love

Lynn X

P.S. See, no names!   —

Dear Lynn

It's probably not a good idea to make comparisons. We never know what's going to happen, or which is the right direction.

And I'm not completely ignorant, I do know her name! Rachel Whiteread's doing great right now but in ten years' time could be ... I don't know ... knocked sideways by the death of her kids, say, in a car accident. With her driving, and escaping injury!

Don't be so dramatic. You're on your own path.

I can tell, I'm your mother.

You're the most strong-willed, independent creature on the planet.

From Sparkhill, anyway!

Must be a good few others like you in London, stands to reason. Whiteread for one.

I've never even begun to do the things I wanted to, yet I still have fun.

Chin up,

Love

M XX

M
How's it going?
L xx

[Wrote this on a 1920s postcard of Niagara Falls, with rings and bangles I had cut out from an Argos catalogue and collaged at the base of the waterfall. Someone had told me that thousands of couples get engaged every year on the walkway above the drop, exchanging rings, most of which might as well be thrown straight into the void.]

—

Dear Lynn
Yeah, I'm doing all right, considering.
I'm more-or-less manager of The Blind Traveller on the four nights I work there.
The man of the moment is OK too. So far!
I'm haunted by pictures of that poor black woman, her pretty son murdered at the bus stop by a gang of thugs. Also, those little boys killing another little boy, beside the railway. Can't get my head around any of it, even now, months later.
Not sure why it gets to me. I'm not the maternal type. I don't think.
Suppose it's because the TV and papers hit us over the head with these sorts of stories. You're expected to feel outraged even when you aren't.
Whose fault is it when youths and kids behave like that?
The government. And the public education system, I'd say.
Simpler for them to blame the mothers.
It's not right, though.
Love
M XX

Mother

Turning up for work with Susan after the bullshit of Christmas has cheered me up no end. I love her sharpness. And her head of hair! Tied back most of the time, a revelation when loose.

The Freud piece is nearly ready now, in this version.

Luckily for me, as I've still got a fair amount to do on the video for her Gimpel Fils show, on at the same time. We went out for lunch today, at our usual place, the café down by the roundabout. After our soup we walked over to the Saatchi Gallery. The only work I'd wanted to see was by Jenny Saville. Wasn't disappointed. Luscious, fat self-portraits: naked, electric flesh. Susan liked them too, said they put her mind of Jo Spence's photographs, equally undisguised.

We didn't bother to look at anything else in the exhibition and returned to the studio.

HAPPY NEW YEAR

With love, Lynn

P.S. See if you can get hold of a book from the library on Jo Spence. She's dead now, of cancer, documented in revealing photos of herself. You'd like her. She set up a socialist-feminist collective called the Hackney Flashers!

P.P.S. Sorry, Mum, my letters are all art. Names again too. Such a drag, I know. I don't reckon there's any stopping this now. Nothing else I want to do, in truth. Night and day, making stuff is all I think about. May brand me as a bore. It does, for sure. Not the work, though. My work has to be much much much better than me. Should this happen it will all have been worthwhile.

19 JAN 94

M

House has gone. Bulldozed flat by the Council, tons of rubble removed.

I'm pleased, in a way. It would only have become accepted, forgotten, damaged.

Now the work stands free, as an exceptional memory.

Wonder what Whiteread feels?

L xx

[On a postcard of Tracey Emin and Sarah Lucas in Brick Lane market, holding watermelons beneath their arms, the photo titled *Big Balls*, published for the group show *Hôtel Carlton Palace Chambre 763*, in Paris the previous year.]

20 MAR 94

Mother

The Freud Museum exhibition opened a couple of days ago. Very well received.

Susan made a speech.

Said really nice things about me.

I admire the way she expresses herself, with a sly smile and semi-benign precision. Always thoughtful and original. At one point she said something like: 'My starting points were artless, worthless artefacts and materials – rubbish, discards, fragments, trivia and reproductions – which seemed to carry an aura of memory and to hint at meaning something, something that made me want to work with them, and on them.'

Susan is one of those people who, as they say, commands the room.

Words! I told you, she's good at words.

Gatherings make me queasy, so I wandered off around the museum. On the stairs there's a strange framed oil panting by the Wolf Man

Have you ever been to the Freud Museum?

It's in the house off the Finchley Road where he briefly lived on fleeing Vienna. His analyst's couch is there, covered in a Turkish rug. And that weird leather consultant's chair of his, designed, it says on a label, by the Austrian architect Felix Augenfeld, a present in 1930 from his eldest daughter, Mathilde.

The things you discover running away from the art crowd!

I'll write again soon.

Love

Lynn

28 MAR 94

Mum

I think I've reached the end of working for Susan. It's been wonderful and I've learnt masses from her, but I need to concentrate on my own stuff now. Susan herself has been trying for ages to instil confidence in me about the public worth of my work.

It's been a slow start for me. Maybe things'll pick up speed now.

The show at Gimpel Fils in Davies Street has just started. We're screening our four-and-a-half-minute video loop, more-or-less continuously, on a monitor framed by the gallery's blacked-out street window. The ghostly play of light and shadow, imagined by Susan, was shot by me.

I'm proud of it. Susan is too. We work well together.

In their catalogue, the gallery argued that 'despite the

aesthetic modesty of its straight forward demonstration of light on matter, the video *Bright Shadow* acted as sort of index to the whole exhibition.'

I don't see it.

Quite the opposite.

To me, in working on the video, my template was Susan's *Measure by Measure* series, which she began in 1973 and still makes annually. These customised burettes filled with the year's ashes of her burnt paintings are the soul of the show, to me.

I don't need to quiz her to know that this is so.

Sorry, it's difficult for you to suss what I mean without seeing it all.

It helps me to tell you, all the same. Hope you don't mind too much.

I'm never going to forget the experience of working for Susan.

Do you know what she said the other day, railing against the mania for statistics on 'audience surveys', 'gallery footfall' and the rest of the rubbishy jargon? Susan announced to me, in a newsreader-y voice: 'The Arts Council has awarded record funding to the dynamic new group show *The Art of Audience Surveys*, secured by one hundred per cent audience pre-approval.'

That's Susan!

Much love, Lynn x

—

Dear Lynn
You asked how it was for me having to go out to work when you were small.
It was fine. I wanted to, for the company.
Headquarters telephonist for a taxi firm was the winner.

Better Cars in Bromwich.
Power-trip putting on the headphones and mike. Sat myself up straight! Honestly!
Other mothers were happy to pick you up from school. You were always A1 on your homework.
Did us both good, me to get out of the house and you to be independent, your own person. That's what I say!
Love
M x

19 APR 94

Mum

Not only do you never tell me anything worth hearing about my actual father, you're equally tight-lipped about my so-called stepfathers. Those men who came and went from our house like stray cats. Here today gone tomorrow, some briefly back again, for as long as I can remember. In the end I didn't bother asking them their names.

One of them lasted two years. A record. Nobody was going to beat that.

He wasn't so bad. Hardly saw him. Worked nights at ... Where was it? At the Land Rover plant? I forget.

Smartened up my bicycle. Which was nice.

What went wrong with him? You never said.

Sorry, I'll stop. This is mental. We both know who were the jerks.

One in particular, in my book.

It wasn't your fault.

Love

Lynn

—

Dear Lynn

You do go on. And only half the story.

What about that Gerald bloke, who took us with him on holiday to Berlin?

Some army reunion. Ages ago, before the wall came down. He'd served there, in the military police.

You were amazing. At fourteen. Decoding the guidebooks for us. Insisted we saw everything.

I've never forgotten that collector's museum. Can't now remember what it's called. Loads of Picassos, hundreds and hundreds of his drawings. Your eyes were out on stalks!

From there we walked across a park to the Charlottenburg Palace. Unbelievable, never seen anything like it inside. Didn't know the Germans could be such fun!

Art-wise, I mean.

Complete riot.

Dig up Gerald in your screwy memory and give truth a boost, I'd say!

Love

Mother

12 MAY 94

Mum

I'm shocked how little we were taught at school about the war in the Far East.

Bridge on the River Kwai is the extent of my knowledge on the subject!

My ignorance was on parade yesterday, no mistake.

I had tea at the Photographers' Gallery with a Japanese woman, Tatsuko, who taught Oriental Art at St Martin's. Wasn't prearranged. We happened to be in the gallery at the same time, looking at a devastating exhibition of the H-bombings.

And her story poured out afterwards, over tea in the café. She was born, she told me, in Nagasaki in 1939. Her father was a textile worker and as Japan's involvement in the war escalated, he took her, her mother and elder brother away by train to stay in safety with relatives in the country.

The father returned to the city, to his job in the factory.

After tea, when Tatsuko had left, I took note of her words as accurately as I could remember them. She had spoken in a near expressionless tone, looking steadily out through the window. I can hear Tatsuko's voice in my note of these words, which must be pretty close to what she actually said:

On 9 August 1945, thirty-six thousand residents of Nagasaki were killed, without warning, by the United States releasing from miles high in the sky one massive bomb, despite knowledge of the horrors inflicted by their nuclear attack on Hiroshima three days earlier. Fat Man was the American code-name of the plutonium-explosion bomb detonated above Nagasaki. It terminated in agony my father's life.

Accounts by survivors of atrocities move me. Physically, in my stomach. In my legs, sometimes forcing me to stamp my feet. It's something I'd like to express in film, one day.

Obliquely.

Love

Lynn

P.S. Oh, yes, as well as Alec Guinness in *BotRK*, there's Marguerite Duras and *Hiroshima Mon Amour*. I've read that. It's a beautiful book, and moving about the war. No desire to see the movie, despite my crush on Resnais.

Mum
Another question. No idea how or why this shot into my head.
When I was...I don't know, about ten...I had a small autograph book with pastel-coloured pages.
Do you remember?
Mystery to me who gave me the book, or who wrote this in it – always stuck in my mind:
Good better best
Never let it rest
Until your good is better
And your better best.
I'd like to give him a punch on the nose! Guarantee it was a him!
Who was it? Can you remember?
Love
Lynn xx

9 JAN 96

Mum
Haven't thought about this for ages – why don't I have any godparents?
Lynn xx

[Written on one of many typographic postcards I still own, designed and printed by Daniel Eatock, who lived in Stoke Newington at the time, not far from my flat. This card reads: *Say yes to fun and function and no to seductive imagery and colour!*]

—

Dear Lynn

You're not too old to take a bit of advice from your mother, are you?

Don't take offence.

It's just that you do yourself no favour plucking your eyebrows to extinction.

I know I've told you this before and you take no notice. I won't mention it again, I promise.

Ask Susan Hiller what she thinks.

Bet she agrees with me.

Mother x

14 FEB 96

Mum

You're my valentine!

Hah! Hah!

How many of my drawings have I sent you now? Quite a few. This one's in my semi-architectural style.

Don't draw so much these days. Three or four years ago I shifted focus. Onto film. Video is the fashion, but I adore film: 16 mm, shot on a hand-cranked Bolex camera I borrowed ages ago from St Martin's. Sort of permanently, it appears. There's this incredible texture shooting on a Bolex, almost tactile, so that film becomes object as well as image.

I'm obsessed!

Possessed!

Much love

Lynn

P.S. How do you know I pluck my eyebrows hard? Does it show in one of the photos I've sent you?

P.P.S. Though I'm glad you seem to have forgiven me

for not wanting to come up to Sparkhill, I'm not absolutely sure quite what's going on in that weird head of yours. Not that I understand my own much better. All these years, ten now, that we haven't seen each other. With sort of explanations from me, and plenty of failed attempts to fully clarify it all to myself. No real conversation between us, though. No concerted attempt by you to persuade me to change my mind. Strange. And strange that neither of us seem too bothered.

—

Dear Lynn
I'd realised film was becoming your thing.
Not in the least surprised. On holiday you were always the one to take the best pictures. Not me.
I've got one here, beside my bed. On the beach at Southport. Remember? You couldn't have been more than twelve.
You've always done everything well.
Except cooking!
Love
Mother

28 FEB 96

Mum
What I do I do OK. Don't do enough, that's my trouble. Takes me ages to commit.
No stopping me once I've started!
Nothing with me is ever light-hearted. Since taking to film it's occupied most of my time. Check daily for film on numerous TV channels. Buy hundreds of cheap VHSs from China.
Relentless?

Yes, I'm content to be called relentless.
Lynn xx

P.S. I'm a sort-of perfectionist, for some reason. I'm not sure why. Certainly not your fault that I so dislike getting things wrong. You've never made those kind of demands on me. Odd that I turned out like this. Can't bear making mistakes in anything I do. Going in the wrong direction on the tube. Forgetting to buy cat food. That's before I even begin to make a film!

27 MAR 96

Mum

I once mentioned to you Compston of Factual Nonsense and the Shoreditch events he organised. His funeral was last week. Found self-dead in his bed. Only twenty-five. Never spoken to him myself. Sad all the same.
Turk and Hume painted his coffin.
Sarah S. was a friend and says she's pretty sure it was a mistake. He had serious money problems, unable to sleep, and had developed a habit of sniffing liquid ether to send him out. Exactly what it did!
At his second Fête Worse Than Death, in Hoxton Square the year before last, Sarah and Georgie dressed up as nurses and together ran a stall they called Anarchy Hospital. On the grass nearby, Emin invented a terrific game, Rat Roulette, giving out fun prizes she'd made herself!
It's true, I had my doubts about Compston. He was a force for change, though, and I'll miss his presence on the scene.
X Lynn X

Mum

Yesterday I took a couple of my films in to show the ICA, hoping they'd put them into one of their Experimental Shorts evenings.

No such luck.

Different luck instead! In the ICA bookshop they were selling some handmade Emin things for twenty-five pounds.

I bought one! To go with her T-shirt.

So appealing. She's glued onto brown cardboard a colour snap of her and her twin brother as kids, beside a mini Christmas tree and enormous pile of wrapped parcels. Emin has written in black ink on the back:

With our life in our hands

Paul do you remember the mercury, we'd sit at the top of the stairs – 4 flights – shining and wooden – We'd roll the mercury out the bottle – tiny little silver balls, forming and re-forming – And us at the bottom of the final flight – taking it in turns. Ready with hands open, to catch the tiny silver drops.

Looking back, I think we've been lucky

Very lucky

Tracey Emin 1996

With masking tape she's stuck an A-shaped piece of wire to the back, to hang it up by. It's here on the kitchen wall right now, beside the Rio's monthly film programme. Looks great!

Love

Lynn

21 JULY 96

Dear Mum

This is the flyer which Sam's Place has printed for my first ever solo show!

I wrote the text, mostly. Harder work than making the film!

A tiny gallery, in an old shop, with the original wooden floors and cream-painted tongue-and-groove kickboards around the walls. Half a dozen people max can watch the film at one time.

It's in Soho, with a cool café next door, where I sit in the window and read, drink coffee and eat banana cake, watch people go in and out of the gallery, try to see in their faces when they leave what they thought of my film I intended to call to see you when I was doing the shoot but I was with people.

Another time.

I know, I say that but haven't been home since heading off for St Martin's. Two hours away on the train to Birmingham International and twenty minutes local bus to Sparkhill.

Things are going so well, making things, I'm afraid to break the spell. There's always so much I want to do, that I can do down here in London.

It seems being separated from you has done me good. A cliché, but some things become clichés because they're true.

We'll see, we will see.

I'll never be able to explain.

With love

Lynn

LALAGE N.R. LYNGH
A film by
Lynn Gallagher
Sam's Place, 79 Beak Street, W1F 9SU
0171 494 1889
Wed to Sat 12.00 to 6.00

This short film – eighteen minutes – is a fictional documentary about the disappearance of a schoolgirl artist, told through a collage of black and white images, still and moving. The fractured narrative begins in the art room at her comprehensive, with work which could be hers pinned to the wall, where the interview with her art teacher – a woman – takes place. 'Lalage', the teacher says, 'was a raw talent, the translator of feelings into form.'

The head teacher – a man – speaks of his regret at the loss of a pupil of potential. There are shots of girls in the gym, straddle jumping the box, climbing ropes. Jump cuts of empty parks and abandoned sweet shops and the public library at night, in Sparkhill, where Lalage lived. Teenage hands slowly turn the pages of a book. The whistles of many trains, synchronised.

The narrative is unclear – as life is, especially when you are sixteen. Although Lalage has, to all intents and purposes, disappeared into thin air, leaving behind bewildered teachers, classmates and parents, there is no suggestion that she might be dead.

Lynn Gallagher studied at St Martin's College of Art, graduating in 1988, winner of the Richardson Prize for Drawing. In the early 1990s she was attracted to the film-work of Chris Marker, to his unique combination of radical content and experimental technique, and to Derek Jarman's exuberant use of Super 8. Gradually, film replaced drawing as her primary means of expression.

She has contributed several filmic series of still photographs to group exhibitions, in Manchester, Glasgow and Stuttgart. This is the first solo public showing of completed film work by Gallagher. Although Gallagher herself was brought up in Sparkhill, a Birmingham suburb, her film *Lalage N.R. Lyngh* is no more than tangentially autobiographical.

25 JULY 96

M

You won't believe this! My film has been bought by Saatchi!
Perfect birthday present!
L xx

[When sorting through this correspondence it became clear that the words I used were often augmented and explained by the captions and images of the postcards I wrote them on. Over the years I have gathered and kept thousands of postcards, some new, some old, a number physically transformed by me through collage, incisions, paint and other techniques. On this occasion I open-posted Mum a card designed and published the previous year by John Bevis at his Coalport Press in Shropshire, on the picture-side of which he printed the phrase, in black lettering on gloss white ground: *Art isn't working – A postcard from the Saatchi Collection.*]

—

Lynn
How dare you? All those personal things out in the open without asking my permission?

You've got a nerve, girl. The cheek.
Let any of your art lot near me and I'll tell them a thing or two
about their precious little one-day wonder.
Try me. Just try me.
Mother

4 AUG 96

Keep your hair on, Mum! It's my story as much as yours!
I haven't said anything wrong anyway. Haven't 'said'
anything much at all, it's mostly images. And sound.
Recorded sound, manipulated to make a sort of music.
The elements which matter to me are the visual and the
musical. Words are a sideline, in brackets.
Calm down and give it a second go.
Lynn

[Sent on a *Dance With Me – It's Not Over* postcard, the
colour photograph of a record on the turntable against
a sky blue ground, published by the Terrence Higgins
Trust for free distribution to promote understanding of
AIDS.]

—

L
Maybe I overreacted. I reserve judgement!
M x

[Written by Mum on one of her store of standard, blank
Post Office postcards.]

Mum

Here's copy of a wonderful review which will be in the up-coming issue of *Art Monthly*.

I've got myself a dealer, Bridget Mansfield. She invited me out to lunch to say she's intrigued by my work and wants to represent me. An unusual modern art dealer, frumpy in looks and based in Southwark, with not another dealer in sight. Except that Tate Modern is due to open in 2000 in the nearby power station!

Mansfield Art operates from two floors of a Regency building which she and her husband bought for a song twenty years ago. I like her, believe her when she says she sees her job as helping me do and be and make whatever I want, whenever I need to.

Bye for now.

L xx

[The review wasn't with the letter. Mum may have sent it on to Aunt Betty.]

18 SEPT 96

Mum

Did you have to have write such stupid questions about my film?

I preferred your anger to the praise.

Of course it's based on me. Everything always is, even when it isn't, if you see what I mean. Everyone's always is. Films, novels, the lot

I mean, *The Magic Snowman* or *The Good, The Bad and The Ugly* or *Jules et Jim* or *An Artist of the Floating World* or *The Handmaid's Tale* ... I could go on.

They respond to or react against personal experience. If they didn't, they'd be shit.

Lalage N.R. Lyngh is not a direct reflection of what happened to me. Too hazy and distant to connect to fact. I'm there though, from beginning to end. Backstage.

Obscurity not disguise.

Making this film, and the public's embrace of it, has altered and therefore anticipated my future. In a sense.

If that makes sense.

Does to me, anyway.

Lynn xx

6 NOV 96

Mum

I really do dislike the word 'collector'. Everyone thinks you must be great if you're a so-called 'serious collector'. Wrong!

They tend to be major-rich, mean, grasping, possession-mad, controlling, self-satisfied ... MEN mostly. If women, the indulged wives and daughters of patrician wealth. I hate myself for letting Saatchi buy *Lalage*.

That's what happens. You're shut away in the exhibitionless dark and when the light is suddenly switched on, you're blinded, and agree to anything the man with the money wants. In no time you're caught, hostage to the market.

Not me, I promise!

Luckily, I've never cared about money. Never had it, never wanted it. No desire to spend a single social moment in its vicinity.

Enough to make my work and to feed the cat, that's all I need.

Hard though I try to deny it, I've got to admit it's another

similarity to you, this disregard for money.
Different reasons, same effect.
Love
Lynn

—

Lynn
Where do you dig up these ideas?
I'm not anti-money, not in the least. I've always wanted to
hobnob with the rich. Never had the chance, that's the problem.
I do agree with you on one thing. They take right bloody good
care to keep the rest of us out. Once you've got it, keep it, that's
the fat man's rule. By any means you fancy, legal or not.
I'd be the same, I'm sure.
Love
Mother

28 NOV 96

Mum
You think my stuff's odd, what's-the-point-ish, I know
you do!
Well you should have been with me last night on the
South Bank for Stockhausen's Helicopter Quartet.
He's amazing. Anything's possible and everything
permitted.
This was the filmed version, with the Arditti Quartet
videoed playing in four separate helicopters flying
through the sky, projected onto screens in the Queen
Elizabeth Hall, below which the same four musicians
performed on stage in live synchronisation, the com-
poser seated in the centre of the auditorium at a large
sound-control desk.

Terrific music!

Stockhausen wrote something fun in an essay about his childhood: 'I think that, being dead, my parents gave me much more support than they would have in life.'

I love all that. No rules!

With love

Lynn

15 JAN 97

Look, Mum, let's repair the damage.

Try to.

Lynn xx

[One of a series of postcard works in which I painted back in acrylic Gordon Matta-Clark's architectural removals, in this case on a later black and white postcard from the Art Institute of Chicago, of the wooden framed house which he split down the middle in 1974.]

—

Leave off will you, Lynn, I haven't the energy. Just stop. We don't have to do this. Forget about it and get on with your life. Let me get on with mine.

It'll sort itself out, given time and peace.

Or it won't.

Who cares?

Mother

[On another of her standard PO postcards.]

Mother

Want to let you know that Bridget is putting on a show of my work later this month. I'll send you the details when they come through.

Also been approached by Artangel, who commission work in unusual buildings. Asked me what I might like to do. Can't think right now. Need to come up with something good, as I'd love to work with them.

They've been going since the 1980s. It was Artangel which made possible Whiteread's *House*.

See you.

Love

Lynn

Mum

Crap! Bridget's Press Release, enclosed. Can't believe she didn't show me a draft before xeroxing hundreds of copies and posting them out.

My first reaction was to assume she must've printed out someone else's blurb by mistake!! Doesn't relate in any sensible way to my work!

I've warned Bridget that if she insists on this ridiculous art-world practice of mass mailouts of meaningless guff, I'm off. With me she'll need to be personal. Invite potential buyers to tea, maybe. Two, three at a time. Send individual letters to selected media, offer exclusive use of certain images.

Give a private view if she must but don't expect me to turn up.

I didn't this time and won't in the future.

Why would I want to bump into people I dislike? And
see people I do like in a loud crowd where I can't hear
what they say?
Your angry daughter
XX

MANSFIELD ART
18 Union Street, London SE1
Lynn Gallagher
Let's Wait a Moment
18 March to 30 April 1997
Tues to Fri 10.00am to 6.00pm;
Sat 10.00am to 1.00pm

Mansfield Art is pleased to present their first exhibition
of the work of Lynn Gallagher, encompassing four technically diverse filmic explorations undertaken during the
last decade, affirming the talent displayed in her acclaimed release last year of the notoriously mysterious
semi-autobiographical short film *Lalage N.R. Lyngh.*

The rich variety of subject in the work of Lynn Gallagher
defies definition, a reminder that the forces that shape
nature are more powerful – and will last longer – than
us. The contested surfaces of her films, often elegant
and minimal as well as baroque and bombastic, point to
a magical material transformation: the crystallization of
movement into form.

Riven through with Gallagher's inimitable humour and
rigour, this exhibition is in itself a phenomenological and
psycho-spatial experience, an attempt to materialise
uncertainty.

Lynn Gallagher was born in Birmingham in 1965 and studied for her BA at St Martin's College of Art, where she won the Richardson Drawing Prize. Her work has been seen in several prestigious group shows, including New Contemporaries, British Art Show and Manchester Independent, and, in 1996, presented in a solo show at Sam's Place, in Soho.

—

Lynn
Makes no sense to me. It wouldn't, would it? I'm not meant to understand. Keep it in the club, make art a privilege.
Probably means sod all!
I don't mind. If it earns you a living.
Mother x

[Mum wrote this on a commercial colour postcard of the auditorium at Birmingham Rep, the theatre we used to go to, now and again.]

29 MAR 97

Mother
Proof that I'm right!
There've been brief mentions in *Time Out*, *Dazed & Confused* and a local mag called *What's On in South London*. The only serious review I've seen is this one I'm sending you, from *The Guardian*, the result of my friend Philip taking with him to see my show his friend Darien Ebony, the paper's new art critic.
Connections, yes. Actual, though, not bought. No spin-offs in any direction.
Take it as it is. I am the work and have nothing more to

say. If I did, I'd have said it, in the work.
Sorry to go on. Thanks for being there.
Love
Lynn xx

The Guardian
Darien Ebony 27.03.1997
Lynn Gallagher. *Let's Wait a Moment*
Mansfield Art, 18 Union Street, London SE1

Lynn Gallagher is an unusual artist, in a number of respects. She is secretive both about the means of making and about the meanings of her films, eschewing the standard – and mistaken – practice of today's fashionable artists to explain to extinction. Gallagher is also passionate, driven by personal need to make original works of art, a woman who appears knowledgeable rather than knowing.

The result is these two immensely refreshing short films and two fascinating photographic projects.

Negative Photographic Works is a series of still images, catalogued by Mansfield Art as 'cross-processed slide film printed as cibachromes mounted on aluminium'. The juxtaposition of doll-like figures and similarly dressed women in negative and positive colour is disturbing, with its mother and daughter allusions. *We The People*, a black-and-white film, is equally unsettling, shot in an eerie model village in Winchester, influenced by Gallagher's immersion in *The Devils of Loudun*, the Aldous Huxley novel as well as Ken Russell's film of the same title, designed by Derek Jarman. As often is the case with her films, sound is crucial, here sampled from the tracks of period films in which lynch mobs chase down fugitives, as if through the empty streets of the model village.

Sordal emerged by happenstance from a visit to Norway, when Gallagher decided she needed to find and film a hermit living in the wilderness. In fact, in the search she found an abandoned film set in remote surroundings, which became the main subject of her film.

Human Camera [also known as *Mouth Pictures*] resulted from an obsessive desire described in Gallagher's own words: 'All I can say is that I wanted to keep the pictures that went inside me.' She purchased three metres of thick black cloth in Shepherds Bush Market and made a big bag, which loosely covered her body to the waist, pointed at the top like a Ku-Klux Klan hood. Then she prepared light sensitive paper at home, at night, perched inside her wardrobe, cutting it to the shape and size of her mouth and storing the pieces in a light-tight box. With bag and box, she walked down to a local park, put the black bag over her head, opened the box inside in the dark, fitted the paper between her teeth and then, not knowing quite what her mouth, the camera, might see, emerged from the bag and took a photograph. The images shown here in the exhibition are blurred and red, coloured by her blood, bathed in the ethereal red light of her body, surrounding indecipherable landscapes and fragmented figures.

This is the work of a true creator.

30 MAR 98

M

Wanted to tell you how really wonderful it is for me to read in public that someone I've never met has paid such attention to my work. That he finds in my films and photos what I hoped might be seen.

L XXX

[Much to my surprise, I see that this was written on an invitation postcard to a joint exhibition in Köln by Sarah Lucas and Angus Fairhurst titled *Odd-bod Photography*, illustrating together the self-portrait photographs *Got a Salmon On* (Lucas) and *Stand Still and Rot* (Fairhurst). Bridget must have given it to me, knowing I admire Lucas' work. Can't imagine what impelled me to give it away to Mum. Delighted, twenty years later, to get it back.]

22 MAY 98

Mum
You're always telling me I'm 'full of hate'.
Which I hate, of course!
I just have strong views, maybe exaggerated a bit from time to time to make a point. You have to overstate your case if what you're trying to say is deliberately ignored.
Don't see that I had much choice. Even if it resulted in art-supremos treating me like a madwoman.
You didn't, I'll grant you that.
Your take was that I should keep my thoughts to myself and avoid trouble. Like you do, you said.
Except you don't. Don't avoid trouble, I mean.
Frankly, I prefer my kind of trouble to yours.
Never mind.
'Never mind', another of your phrases. What am I, a fucking parrot?
Lynn

P.S. I do HATE puffer coats, that's for sure. And puffer

jackets. Men's and women's. Hate the word puffer. Ugly! Errchh! Why do the people who wear such hideous things insist on looking so pleased with themselves?

2 DEC 98

Mum

I had dinner with Betty and Tony in Cambridge last week. After working all day in a specialist film lab attached to The Cavendish.

Beautiful house.

In Chesterton, easy walk from the town centre. You know this. Obviously. Sorry, I'd not been to their new home myself.

Anyway, I quite liked it. Smart without being show-off.

And I've always got on with Tony. He's nice to me. Not sure, but I think he's stopped selling dredging equipment and is now running a building company?

Aunt Betty's mad about purple and blue. Everywhere you look. Carpets, walls, crockery, flowers in the back garden, wisteria covering the front.

Not for me, white's my thing. Do very much like her doing it, though.

Your sister turned out OK. Pity about her kids!

Love

Lynn

31 DEC 98

M

Ha! Ha!

This is what it's like for artists!

HAPPY NEW YEAR

Me xxxx

[I sent Mum another of my Angela Martin postcards. Leeds Postcards used regularly to publish Martin's cards, including, as seasonal specials, her coloured cartoony drawings of human-like fairies perched at the top of Christmas trees. This one crossly says: *Seasonal work, long hours, low pay, no "health and safety", no danger money... They said I could keep the dress...*]

—

Lynn, dear. The whole world, you know, doesn't revolve around you artists.
Do you ever think of anybody but yourself?
Leyland Trucks has been taken over by the Americans and hundreds of men on the estates in Sparkhill laid off. Without the custom, shops are closing. My hairdresser's moving across into Moseley.
That's local.
What about peace in Belfast?
Not a word from you about the Good Friday Agreement. And your father was half Irish. The better half.
Burst the art bubble and get a life!
Love from Mother

19 JAN 99

Mother
Dad 'was' ... Is he dead?
Lynn

P.S. Agree: artists are as ordinary as everyone else.

[On a National Gallery postcard of Andrea Mantegna's *Agony in the Garden*.]

Dear Lynn
Far from it. He's in prison, in Barcelona. Due out soon.
Did I tell you I've a new man? He's nothing much to look at but seems a decent sort. A solicitor. Works for a firm of debt collectors in the Balti Triangle. Indian on Indian.
He's not. Pale skin, dyed blond hair.
They believe in him more than they do in themselves.
I believe him too.
Could easily be wrong. Poor form when it comes to men, have to admit.
Should have gone the other way and loved women.
Maybe not.
Mother xxx

2 FEB 99

M
Do you think I look like you?
I do. Nobody else does.
You'll have been prettier than me when you were my age.
L XXX

[Wrote this on a spare Doom of Youth postcard designed and printed by John Stalin – a pseudonym? – of a mechanical metal figure striding across the earth, with a male body wearing striped pyjamas tucked under its arm and the caption *This Man Has Been Raped By A Women's Lib Robot*.]

Mum

I'm a bit worried about you. No verifiable reason.

Maybe because you've not been writing to me much.

Are you eating properly? You used to cook so well, always making us lovely meals. You being a good cook is one of the reasons I'm not, I expect.

Stupid of me, I know.

Loads of artists like food. That Matta-Clark bloke ran a café in New York as a work of art and invited his artist-friends to design the meals!

A prolific Swiss-born artist described his studio method as like being in a kitchen, seeing himself as a 'Sugarbomb maker ... When you've got a nicely set pudding like that, a cake, and pour chocolate over it. And then cream on top of that. The more you put on the sweeter and nicer it gets.'

I like it when I learn that artists I admire were good at other things. Everyday things, like windsurfing, or knitting. It annoys me when the press makes them into cardboard heros.

Some do it to themselves. Unforgivably.

Look after yourself, if you can.

With love

Lynn x

18 JUNE 99

Mum

You've probably heard from Aunt Betty that we had a slap-up lunch together before she caught the Eurostar to her canal holiday in Amsterdam. She's in pretty good nick, your sister.

I took her to The Wolseley in Piccadilly, not long open, already one of those places where the smart-arty set like to be seen. Betty spotted Jeffrey Archer. Me, I've no idea what the berk looks like, glad to say.

Clever menu, very eatable.

Betty told me some family things that I didn't know. She might have been slightly tipsy. Part-drunk on high spirits, first day on holiday from the bank, excited by the society setting. Said something about you having a row with your mum and running off to Blackpool, getting a job as a waitress, all within days of leaving school.

We only managed to get a table because one of the owners is keen on art and has bought two photos of mine.

I'm glad it worked out.

Till soon.

L xxx

26 JULY 99

Mum

This isn't a competition, I accept, but I must have written to you at least four times this year and you've only written to me once.

I don't mind. I'm going to go on writing to you anyway, from time to time, whether you like it or not. About subjects which you may or may not be interested in.

Such as early Wim Wenders movies.

My complete favourite of his is from the mid-1970s, *Alice in the Cities*, because of its unexpectedness, and because it's both totally convincing and shamelessly contrived. A fiction. A work of art.

This sharp nine-year-old girl is abandoned on a plane by her mother and the young man in the seat beside her feels obliged, reluctantly, to return her to her grandmother. Their trans-European journey together is the film.

I can still see *Alice* scenes play in front of my closed eyes, remembered from ten years ago at the Scala Cinema in Kings Cross.

What I wanted to say is that later, post *Paris, Texas* and *Wings of Desire*, Wenders went badly downhill. Instead of making great movies he's been putting on international shows of his dire photographs.

Do we all sooner or later get to the end of the road, unable to produce the quality which once came naturally? Terrifying.

Wenders gives me the creeps these days and I used to worship him.

There're plenty of other modern German artists and writers made of sterner stuff: Beuys; Herzog; Fassbinder; Bernhard; Wolf; Schneider; Vostell; Kriwet; Kippenberger; Sebald; Darboven.

For starters.

I like making lists. They mean something to me, if not to anybody else!

There we go!

Love

Lynn xx

11 SEPT 99

Dear Mother

I've bought a house!

Pinching myself as I type.

A proper Victorian house, in Dalston.

With all the sales since Sam's Place, Artangel's grant, and the Copthorne Prize, I've masses of money. Relatively. Enough for the backend of Dalston!

An old lady had lived in the house for fifty years, died peacefully at home, and her grandson in America has put it on the market untouched. I'm changing nothing, to begin with, nothing at all. Get it professionally cleaned top to bottom and move in, feel-see see-feel what best to do. An artist-friend is coming to live with me. We've been together for nearly two years now, several nights a week in his flat or mine. He's quiet. You really have to listen when he speaks.

If he does.

Richard's his name. The only properly self-sufficient male I've ever come across.

Re: men – I still don't know anything much about my father.

Wasn't there a garage?

What happened to it?

Don't bother. I'm past caring.

Lynn x

18 SEPT 99

M

Tell me more about this new new-bloke you're with,

Is he really all right?

Sounds a bit of a head case to me.

You turfed out the solicitor quick enough. Or did he dump you?

L xxx

[Forgotten that I used to pick up the occasional American light-switch cover postcard. This one to Mum was a photo of Michelangelo's *David* given the features of Bill Clinton, a rectangular gap at the groin for the switch to protrude and be pressed.]

—

Lynn
Eddie's no better or worse than any of the others. As far as I can tell. To date.
At least he's black, got that going for him. Well, brown.
He's a musician. Plays in a dance band. The clarinet.
Gives me ideas about what I might've done if Dad hadn't died and I'd been able to go on with music.
Drinks too much, that's Eddie's trouble. Turns him into ... Never mind. Good as gold most of the time. Very encouraging to me.
He was hired to play in an art-performance piece at Eastside Projects in Digbeth, on our side of town. So I went along. Fantastic place. Genuine. 'We do not make art for the public, we are the public that makes art.' That's what they say. And mean it.
Eddie said I should become one of their volunteers. And I am now!
It's artist-run and they've made it a rule that each exhibition display is recycled in some form for the next. So us volunteers very carefully take down the shows and stack the materials by type in the store for reuse.
I'm twice the age of most of the others.
Don't give a toss. I love it there.
Mother xx

22 SEPT 99

M
Discovered last week a new postcard artist, Simon Cutts. He designs and prints them himself.
Been around for years, I just hadn't happened on him before.
XX L

[On this self-published postcard, Simon Cutts printed, type-like on the front, the question: *was the Nativity a site-specific installation?* and on the back the address of his shop off Brick Lane, called workfortheeyetodo, also lower case.]

—

L
Very good!
What about this one?
M x

[Mum wrote this on a postcard by Leon Kuhn, self-published, titled *Mad Dogs and Englishmen*, the close-up caricature of the politician John Prescott as a rabid bulldog.]

28 NOV 99

Mum
Sorry not to have been in touch for a bit but I've been exceptionally busy with the Artangel project. They've managed to secure the building I requested, discovered by me years ago on the wander from St Martin's.
Elms Lesters Painting Rooms, tucked in behind the church next to the street of guitar shops off the top of Charing Cross Road.
I'll try and describe it for you.
Fantastic space, purpose-built a century ago to paint scenery for West End theatres, with a narrow wooden side-hinged shutter rising thirty feet from pavement to a gantry, through which to haul in and out stage-wide canvas backdrops.

The interior has different levels and open wooden stair-cases. Inspiring!

It's been empty for some time and the owner accepted Artangel's offer for a short-term let. Long enough to give me time to design, film and mount an installation, and record the sound.

I've called my piece *Sea Change Scene*. They're publishing four illustrated essays, printed individually, each presented in a buff graphic folder open at the top, with finger cuts to ease access. Should be good. Not back yet from the printers in Holland. Here's copy of the typed manuscript of one of the texts, written by my key assistant, an Artangel girl whom I hadn't met before, fresh from art school.

Lots still to do.

With love

Lynn

Working with Lynn Gallagher:
my *Sea Change Scene* experience
by Maisie Winnicott

The complexity of Lynn Gallagher's imagination places considerable pressure on her assistants – she is so very demanding on herself that, however hard we worked, it was never quite good enough. This was at first disconcerting, even actively alienating, but, for me at least, the sheer quality of Gallagher's ideas and her utter integrity won me over, and I ended up having the time of my life.

Gallagher instilled in me the sense of necessity to get every single detail right when showing art to the public. She spoke of our obligations to the viewer, of their seminal role in the process of creativity. 'We must never skimp,' I remember her saying in her quiet voice, at lunch in a worker's café around the corner from Elms Lesters. 'Nobody's obliged to come and look. They deserve our best efforts.'

Curiously, the film-work was relatively straightforward: an overlay of separated images in colour and black-and-white, patterns and shapes which gave the impression of unrolling and rolled canvases, of different sizes and form and subject. We blacked out the windows and skylight, removed all recent furnishings, and let collaged film invade, indeed conquer the space. Gallagher was consciously influenced in this work by her intimate involvement with co-making Susan Hiller's film *Bright Shadow*, when she was her part-time studio assistant earlier in the decade.

From an assistant's point of view, the most complicated element of *Sea Change Scene* was the precise high placing and focus of film projection boxes around the place and construction of the sound, with multiple speakers designed to envelop and, on occasion, overwhelm the audience.

We went to an incredible variety of unlikely sources in finding the 'music', as Gallagher referred to the sounds she sought, often related, in her mind, to the scene painters and prop makers who once worked in the building: sawing of wood, banging of nails, brushing of paint, cutting canvas, turning rollers, scrubbing, spraying, scraping. And the noises also of the men themselves: coughing, walking in hobnail boots across the wooden floors, laughing, snatches of pre-War song, drinking tea, spitting, lighting cigarettes and the soft wheeze of them dragging the smoke into their lungs and breathing it out. The whole experience was so powerful because it worked, one hundred per cent. It helped, of course, that

I came to like and admire Gallagher as a woman. What mattered, though, the only thing that matters, is that together we created something which had never before existed and that she is the only person in the world who could have made happen. *Sea Change Scene* is heart and soul Lynn Gallagher.

—

L
Wow! Is that you?!!
I'm impressed.
Good luck when it opens next week.
M XX

[Mum sent me this on a great colour postcard of Mrs Thatcher in the US, standing at a rostrum delivering a speech to the Republican Senatorial Inner Circle in 1993.]

12 DEC 99

Thanks a lot, Mum. Yes, the response to *Sea Change Scene* has been fantastic.
Artangel are great to work with, amazingly generous with both financial and physical support, the show itself wonderfully staffed. They're over-keen on controlling, but no match for me in that department!
You wouldn't believe the inefficiency of some London art galleries, how many are closed when they advertise being open. Depressing disservice to the artists exhibited. Artangel are the opposite.
They didn't at all mind my refusal to attend the private view. Nor did they object to turning down on my behalf requests for mindlessly promotional interviews by

newspapers, radio and TV. I'm fed up with the over-explaining of everything, fuelled by the self-importance of today's rash of media 'experts'. Leave us in the audience to make up our own minds, please!

Too many artists and writers – Gormley, McEwan, Rushdie, Kapoor, Perry, etc. – are desperate to drop a public quote on any subject anybody happens to ask them about.

Personally, I don't see why my views should be more valuable than those of any other woman of my age, just because I'm a maker of toast-of-the-moment art-films.

All Hail Artangel!

L xxx

16 DEC 99

Mum

Very strange feeling: yesterday I met my father for coffee.

He had seen some of the coverage of my show and contacted Artangel. Perhaps foolishly, I rang the number he had left with them and we arranged to meet. At the YMCA off Tottenham Court Road, in the coffee shop, three minutes' walk from Elms Lesters.

I recognised him instantly, though I last saw him when a young child, and had no real idea what he looked like. He was more affluently dressed than I expected, in suede shoes. Still-dark hair smartly cut.

Nothing happened. He said nothing of the remotest interest.

After half an hour I told him, quietly, clearly, that I never wanted to see him again and that if he ever tried to make contact, I'd call the police.

Love, Lynn

—

Lynn. I really don't want to hear any of this.
Keep it to yourself, please, if you don't mind.
Mother xx

[Written on a blank Post Office postcard]

22 DEC 99

Mum

The first thing we've done at No. 28 is build some bookcases, on a suitable wall in every single room. Our bathroom too. And what will be the main spare bedroom.

With a house of my own I've become conscious how important books are to me. Physically. The sight of them on my shelves, the knowledge that when I'm not there, they are, in the place assigned. It matters to me that I own them. Books never desert you. If you take care of them, they pay you back, by existing in your room, perpetually open-able. By you.

I've never counted them. Richard's interleaved his books with mine. Alphabetically, within subject. Joint total of three or four thousand, I'd have thought. Contemporary fiction is my thing, philosophy and politics his. Neither of us read biographies. My side-subject is feminism, books which Richard is equally keen on. Loads of stuff on art, of course.

Part of my anger as a teenager was the struggle against ignorance. I knew that I didn't know, knew that I didn't even know what it was that I needed to know.

I blamed you rather than myself. Thanks for taking that! The anger gradually faded. Or became more focused, maybe. Shifted to being against the hypocrisy of the art world instead of anti-Mum.

I'm wildly antagonistic to the status quo. Livid at the illicit power of money. Of money beyond money. The stench of excess.

Well, I'm forming a strategy. Soon be ready to kick them in the guts!

Lollard Lynn!! xxx

3 JAN 2000

Mum

A new-century present. This is a Gillian Wearing postcard which I've altered by rubbing out the message written on an A4 piece of paper by the man holding it up.

You know she's from Birmingham? Brother and her were brought up by their lone mother.

She was at Chelsea when I was at St Martin's. I love what she does.

Lynn xx

P.S. Small writing to get it all on the message side of the postcard!

[Sent in an envelope, unusually for me. This is one of my best altered postcard pieces. Wearing's title for this series, printed on the back: *Signs That Say What You Want Them To Say And Not Signs That Say What Someone Else Wants You To Say.*]

—

Dear Lynn

I've a present for you too. Better late than never.

It's about your father. All the facts I know. The feelings, I'll keep to myself.

He was tall, wiry, with thick black hair and snow-white skin. A tale-teller from the start, keeper of his own secrets. He said we were born in the same month, two lions, a year apart. Probably not true.

I was already twenty-four, keen to have a baby, and you came along pretty quick.

Your dad worked at the garage when I met him. Owned it, he said. Even before we were married I did the books, unpaid, working in the evenings after my job in the laundry. There was paperwork he kept to himself and I never knew any company details. Ownership, land lease, that kind of thing. I assumed it had belonged to his father, before he retired to the Costa del Sol a year or two before.

Blew up in my face after your dad scarpered to his dad in Spain. God knows what they'd done. Something seriously not right. Two spivvy blokes turned up within days of him leaving. Poked around the place one afternoon without a word to me. The three vintage motors in the back garage were registered in my name. Part of some scam, I expect. They were all I had. And the house, bought and mortgaged by me, luckily. I managed to explain to the bank, and to the police, that the whack of money he owed – to a number of people, it turned out, one from Florida – was nothing to do with me.

Within a month of his disappearance I'd sold the old autos and walked out of the garage. Didn't bother to lock up. Six months later it was pulled down, and a boot camp gym built in its place.

They're all criminals, I reckon. It's all connected. A network.

He didn't try to explain. Cut me out of his life as if I didn't exist. You too, little one. Ditched you too. At first his father answered the phone when I rang. Never said much. Until he got himself a new number, ex-directory. I've never known the address.

What else?

I was stupid, I should have sold the house back then too, along with the cars, and made a complete break for it. I stayed and the two of us made ourselves an OK home. In recent years I've thought, hoped, you'd come back.

There's nothing for you in Sparkhill, I understand that now. I'll ring the estate agent tomorrow. Take whatever I can get and buy a flat. Not far away. Closer to the shops.

I'll be fine. I'm always OK.

Love

Mother x

8 JAN 00

Oh, Mum, what a shit! I'd no idea. He told me he was in international finance!

Yes, I left too, but at least I've kept in touch. Listened to you, even to things I didn't want to hear.

I'm so sorry you had such a bad time. You didn't deserve it.

You'll be better now when you get the flat. Make it small, no spare room, and those useless men you get caught up with won't be able to move in!

Keep in touch

Lots of love

Lynn

9 JAN 00

Mum

Wanted to add that I'm grateful to you for letting go the

question of our very odd habit, as I suppose it's become, of not seeing each other. My reasons for behaving as I do grow more obscure and crazier year by year. I used to be convinced that I more-or-less understood why. By now I'm certain I haven't a clue!

It's good that you're the kind of character who simply gets on with things. I'm lucky to have inherited from you this capacity too.

It won't always be like this. Something will happen to change the pattern, I know it will.

No idea when or how.

One day, one day.

With my love

Lynn

16 JAN 00

Mum

That's another plus about living in London: all the films to be seen.

For fifteen years now I've seen two movies in one night on two different evenings a week.

Except when I'm travelling, or work intervenes.

Mostly at the National Film Theatre, which screens eight different films every single day in their four cinemas. Means I've seen three thousand movies, more or less, over these years.

Explains a lot! To say nothing of all the films watched on TV and VHS.

Always great prints at the NFT. No ads. Films both old and current. Regular special screenings prior to public release, often with the director present for questions.

Remember listening live to Werner Herzog tell his off-set stories. About cooking and eating his own boot after losing a bet. On another occasion, jumping into a giant cactus to amuse, and thank, a cast of dwarves. Such a performer!

Derek Jarman, beaming through his terminal illness, assuring an earnest interviewer that no, not at all, he hadn't felt isolated in any way as a gay schoolboy. 'Everyone was always round at our house', I remember him saying. Or something like it.

Jarman! Irresistible!

I'm talking to myself again. Apologies.

Sort-of nervous chatter, avoiding the subject of you and my father.

Dad.

What kind of 'Dad' has he ever been to me?

My father, your husband. Fuck!

I can tell you, I'm never getting married!

Love

Lynn

—

Darling girl

You sound full of beans. Are you eating properly?

Ha! Ha!

As rich as the Pope now, not surprising you're so pleased with yourself.

Spare a thought for the drug addicts, I say. You see youngsters out of their minds all over the place here these days. Sparkhill, den of iniquity. Plus dogs. Half of them with fat shiny dogs, sharing a blanket. Are the dogs on crack too? The family next door, where your friend Christine used to live, their son sleeps with other druggies in a camp of cardboard boxes down at the back of Argos, not two miles from his home.

Tell me, how does that happen?

The reason why you keep away from here, like it's the plague?
Bubonic bitch.
Me, that is, not you.
I'm done.
Your mother.

26 JAN 00

Mum
I wish you wouldn't write to me when you're drunk, can barely read the scrawl. In fact, I wouldn't mind if you didn't write to me at all. You spout such nonsense.
Crap, in fact.
Lynn

[Looking back, I remember being inexpressibly annoyed with her at the time, which is why I wrote these crass words on a card made by me as a student, from a commercial postcard of the head and shoulders of the Queen and the Duke of Edinburgh, the scrolled title Regina at the top replaced by me with the collaged Vagina, and pasted at the bottom the cut-out from a porn magazine of a naked woman with her legs apart, with a mini police car scissored from somewhere else nudging her breast.]

—

Dear Lynn
How many times have I asked you to call me Mother not Mum?
You've managed to step up from Mummy, time at your age to switch now to Mother, please. Do without dear, if you insist, though it's definitely rude not to.
For a change, don't be difficult. Just do what I ask for once.

You've always been a pain, almost from the start. Weren't even four when you emptied that giant carton of washing powder all over the kitchen floor. Snow, you said. Not so long after your father pissed off.

My luck to be saddled with the most argumentative daughter in the West Midlands. Never did a single thing you were told. On principle, regardless of what it was, you later used shout. So exhausting. You still are.

Why can't you be grateful that people like what you do and run with it, the success, while it lasts? Christ, it doesn't happen to many, such luck.

Must rush. Your Aunt Betty's coming over for dinner and I've got to shop.

She's been staying with Susannah, who's moved again, to Worcester. Been promoted, to Sainsbury's supermarket trouble shooter. Always on the hop with a job like that. Are you ever in touch with your cousin? Or her brother? Gordon lives in Leeds, selling life insurance.

I'll get Betty some chicken. Don't care what I eat myself. She's fussy though, always has been. Sister from hell! No, she's all right really. I'll give her your love.

She'll be spending the night, I expect.

Mother

9 FEB 00

Dear Mother

Note: 'dear' as in costly, to me, in emotion.

Work on my studio finished last week. Shortish walk from the house.

Good people, the builders, a family of Sikhs from Woolwich. The father in a white turban with a salt and pepper beard, five sons in blue turbans and boilersuits, black beards. Each son trained by the dad in a different trade: joiner, plumber, electrician, brickie and roofer. They live all together with their wives and children in a defunct dock-office. Big. Self-converted, obviously.

Silent site, no radio, no smoking, no shouting, the old man policing the show. He cottoned on quick that I want to keep things as unchanged as possible, repairing rather than replacing. The second week they were there he said to me, all pleased with himself, pointing to a window latch: 'Rusty, Miss Lynn. We get it spick and span for you!' He speaks in a musical Punjabi accent, with winning shake of the head, his beard in a hairnet.

By the way, I had to bang on about my father because you refused for years to tell me about him. Endlessly fobbed me off with 'It's too upsetting. I can't talk about it now'. He was equally evasive when I did finally meet the man.

Your letter released a lot of stuff. Thank you. Really, thank you.

Love, L XXX

—

Dear Lynn

You're not being fair. I didn't tell you things so as not to upset you. Not just about him personally but about our relationship in general. Which was terrible. The pits. I made such a mistake. Tried to protect my daughter. Grant me that?

Reminds me. About the child issue. It's not sensible for you and Richard to hang around much longer. Apart from the health risks to you, I don't fancy being a geriatric Grandma.

By the way, I'm thinking of doing the wrinkles around my eyes. They're good at cosmetic surgery over in Moseley.

A stitch in time, as they say.

Love, Mother

M

The child issue, as you put it, is not one, not for me.

I've never wanted to be a mother and have always done everything I could to avoid becoming pregnant. This includes commitment now to a sexually monogamous relationship with a man who's had a vasectomy.

End of story.

Except to add that I find the paternity mania of the average conservative man, his regressive need to 'carry on the line', burdensome to say the least. It represents one of the many abuses of women embedded in British society. So there!

L xx

P.S. Another thing I like about Richard, apart from getting himself snipped, is his clothing. He buys by mail all his shirts, jackets and trousers from a bespoke tailor's shop in Holt, close to the coast in Norfolk. Modelled on old fishermen's gear. Made of cotton drill in grey, blue, brown or black. You have to order by post, cheque enclosed. They're beautifully plain, lovely to touch. He also got from them a super-looking black canvas coat, which they discontinued a few years back – Italians stop him in the street to ask where he bought it!

P.P.S. I really like our little garden in winter. With the shoots dying back you can't tell how neglected it actually is. Abandoned snail shells show up at the bottom of the fence. These days I pick them out, especially the small purple and cream striped ones. Wash them in the kitchen sink and lay them out in rows on the outside window sill. Blackbirds scatter them, hoping for food, and I put them all back. In much the same order. Seems I'm a sort of collector, at heart. Perish the thought!

—

Dear Lynn
Did you ever have an abortion?
I was afraid that boy you went around with in the sixth form might knock you up. Did he fancy himself! Wouldn't have thought twice about getting you pregnant, then jumping ship.
I've never had to get rid of ... you know. More by luck than judgement. Would have done, no question. One's more than enough, for one.
I was lucky with you, such a bundle of busy life. Family of kids in a single person!
I've tried to keep up with you but never really managed to.
M xx

—

Dear Lynn
I meant to ask before. What is the art work which Richard does that takes him so long?
I've been trying to think what it might be. Does he make art-watches? Small stitch embroidery? Seems unlikely.
Let me know.
Love
Mother

[A sheet of white paper on which Mum had made strange drawings, in child's crayons, in their way beautiful, of no recognisable form without being wholly abstract. They may have been her idea of embroidery designs.]

20 MAR 00

Mother
Richard chews the printed pages of selected books of psychology and when he has spat enough thick soft paste into a bowl, usually after about three weeks steady mastication, he remakes this into his own paper.
The sheets dry on racks while he puts together from his many notebooks a text randomly selected by the *I Ching*. He then letterpress prints the new book himself in an edition of five, binds it, and guilds the covers in elaborate Celtic scrolls.
I'm joking!
He's a miniature painter, in oil on copper, of futuristic architectural perspectives. Manga-inspired in form, multicoloured in minutest detail.
L XXX

8 MAY 00

My Mother/Mum, MMM for short
Testing! Testing!
How would this idea go down in the West Midlands?
Purchase tax on all luxury goods. High-cost art, jewellery, flash motor cars, five-star hotel rooms, and the rest. The lot. Property too, graduated from ten per cent, say, on the extra above a buyer price of five hundred thousand, rising to fifty per cent on the sum above two million.
Same system for art, starting at forty thousand, I'd recommend. Tax paid direct by the collector. At auction too. It's time for people with money and power to share a chunk of it with the underfed, undereducated and underhoused. With the underprivileged, in one word.

Globally. It can't be so dreadfully difficult to devise a redistributive system of taxation fair to the vast majority of mankind, instead of depositing offensive excess into the pockets of a miniscule minority.

Million-pound price tags on a single piece of contemporary art must, surely, be a grotesque displacement of value?

'I rest my case' I'd say if I was a poncy politician!

Standard socialist stuff, I know.

What I don't understand is why so few people seem to agree that purchase tax on expensive luxuries is a good idea.

Lynn x

—

L

Nobody wants to shell out on the money they've made.
Down on the Algarve they'd crucify you for your proposal!
I read in the Express & Star *that some local ex-pat had thirty million pounds worth of jewellery stolen from her villa in Santa Luzia. Unbelievable! Thirty thousand would be too much!*
Guarantee she's never paid tax. Nor the boss-man funding her.
I'll sign your petition providing you insist that the money made by the government is used to up the state pension.
Wise to butter up the oldies.
More votes to be gained than lost. Numerically. See?
And I'm broke!
M xx

22 MAY 00

M

Doesn't that whole money thing drive you mad? The

ex-pats and their tax havens?

The art world's just as guilty. My journalist friend Lloyd told me the other day that the Frieze enterprise is owned by an outfit registered in tax-nil Jersey and that this in turn is owned by a parent company in the US tax haven of Delaware!

Boxes in boxes within boxes. To avoid tax, yes, and also to dodge scrutiny. To stop me finding out who finances Frieze, how much money they make, and what they do with it. Most of their shareholders' dividends stashed in other off-shore funds, without a doubt!

Must have something to hide. Why else go to the expense of organising this palaver?

Grrrrr!

I hear you growling in unison!

Right?

L XX

—

L

Half-right.

Personally, I don't give a tinker's curse about Frieze. Flim-flam. Irrelevant side-show.

As I say, give us a decent pension. Pay the nurses properly. And the teachers.

Nothing new.

M xx

[Sent on a postcard titled *Sex/Pay Difference*, of twin-like little children, one with a ribbon in her hair, the two standing naked side by side and looking down the front of their nappies, with the caption: 'Oh! That explains the difference in our pay!']

Mother
I've done something most unlike me.
Joined the Neighbourhood Watch Committee.
Don't faint!
And it's not too bad!
I got caught unprepared by a neighbour who sat herself down next to me on the Overground from Dalston Junction in to Liverpool Street. I explained that I didn't really function too well in groups, and she was really nice, said that'll be fine, if I hate it of course I can just pack it in.
'Give it a go,' she said. 'You'd be good for the dynamics of the Committee.'
I've attended most meetings now for six months. Find I like the people. Gives me a ... No, won't say it. Sounds sentimental.
Anyway, I'm a productive member. Find myself voted Chair one of these days!
With love, Lynn

—

Dear Lynn
I've given up smoking, for good this time.
Taken me till mid-July to keep my New Year's resolution.
That's how it goes.
What did it was having this dreadful cough since Easter. In the sun of summer. Mad!
Haven't had a fag now for over three weeks and beginning to realise how much they cost me. In money and health.
Should've listened to you earlier.
Much love, Mother

Mother
I've been away for almost a month, in Cambodia and Laos.
Think I may have come away with some good footage.
We'll see, we'll see.
How're you? Did it snow with you?
It was the cool season in the border mountains, where I was. Still tropical, though. Fewer marauding bugs, that's the main difference. For the last two or three years I've been in touch with this Vietnamese tracker, who's been trying to find a saola for me to film. It's a breed of antelope, extinct everywhere else in the world. The trouble is locating the animal in a secure enough spot where it will still be after I've flown half way round the world, taken a forty-eight-hour train ride and six-day hike into the jungle!
Anyway, it worked this time.
Not sure where I find the physical stamina. The thrill of the chase? Adrenalin? It helps too that I'm thin, sinewy, no redundant flesh.
And very determined!
For someone not remotely sporty, I'm surprisingly agile.
Enough of me. Do write, tell me your news, please.
Love
Lynn

—

Dear Lynn
Double news, saves paper.
I didn't tell you I got married before Christmas. Can't think why. To a two-timing bastard.

*Served a divorce notice on him last week, which may take
months to go through.*
Done. Over. Pretend it never happened.
Set me smoking again, though.
Mother xx

*P.S. I've known him for years. Not as well as I imagined! I
reckon men don't have much choice. They either fancy themselves rotten or slit their throats. Not much in between, so to
speak. He's from the former camp.*

1 FEB 01

Jesus, Mum, will you ever learn?
Does anybody?
About anything?
Lynn

[On a Flying Fish postcard which I must have picked
up in California: a strip-cartoon drawing of a blonde
bombshell with the speech bubble *Well ... if they can put
one man on the moon, why not all of them?*]

20 FEB 01

Dear Mother
I've just been, for the second time, to the best thing any
artist of my generation in London has ever done!
Break Down, it's called. Have you seen it on the news?
Landy's excelled himself this time.
Open free for passers-by to watch the action from close
up. In a vacant C & A store on Oxford Street, him and
a band of assistants in matching overalls are systemat-
ically destroying every single thing Landy owns! An

industrial conveyor belt, with steel rollers, carrying his possessions in a wide circle, to be worked on busily by him and his artist gang. Such a spectacle. Two weeks the job's due to take.

Artangel have published a ring-bound manual naming ,in numbered and categorised lists, all 7,227 of his recycled possessions, including all his artwork, his clothes and a much-loved second-hand Saab car, which he had bought with the proceeds of his first sale to the Tate. It took Landy and a friend off-and-on over a year just to make the inventory!

Don't switch off, Mum! This is more than art, it's life!

Look what his mother wrote:

To: Dear Michael & Gillian. Hope everything turns out great. I hope everything is fine for you. I am so proud of you, as so is your dad. You must be so tired. Gillian said you were enjoying every minute of it. Anyway will see you soon. With love Mum X.

Landy added a simple conclusion to the manual: 'I would like to thank ... Gillian Wearing for loving me and allowing me to use all her possessions.'

With anything good there's always more to say, more of the story to tell.

Patience!

I heard from my friend Georgie that her painter-husband Gary had been upset on hearing about Landy's plan to obliterate a large work, in gloss paint on steel, he had given him as a present not long ago. Gary insisted on taking it back home. Until, on attending the Oxford Street opening, stunned by the guts and spectacle of *Break Down*, he straight away brought the painting back to be deconstructed.

Georgie says that Landy said in an interview: 'Talking about value: the only time I ever thought "Christ what am I doing?" was when I set about blow torching the gloss paint from Gary Hume's painting in front of Canadian and German film crews!'

That's an all right story, you must admit! And it's true!

Love

Lynn

1 APR 03

M

My Camden Arts Centre show opens next week. First large solo in a London public space. They're excited, I'm apprehensive.

Camden publishes a brochure for each of their exhibitions, in a design I've always liked, with wire eyepieces in the spine for box-file storage. This is for you.

With love

Lynn

Lynn Gallagher
Camden Arts Centre
April 9th to June 4th 2003

Throughout the development of any expressive form which they can call their own, visual artists tend to be inspired as much by what they read as what they see. This is unquestionably true of Lynn Gallagher, who has read massively, mostly of twentieth-century European fiction, starting as a child on her weekly visits to the public library in Sparkhill, Birmingham. Contemporary female artists with a similar predilection for reading include Sarah Lucas, who spends as much time with a book by the fireside as she does in her studio, and Fiona Banner, the widely read founder of The Vanity Press.

On moving to London to attend St Martin's College of Art, Gallagher was introduced by her tutors to the still-fashionable philosophical and aesthetic theories of writers such as Giorgio Agamben, Gilles Deleuze and Jean Francois Lyotard. The most forceful influence on Gallagher, however, was the book *Ways of Worldmaking* by Nelson Goodman, teacher of analytic philosophy at Harvard University and a substantial collector of contemporary art. Goodman's comment 'Worldmaking as we know it always starts from worlds already on hand, the making is always a remaking' resonates all along the line of Gallagher's films which, despite their breathtaking inventiveness, are rooted in the objects and experiences of her actual life – as everything always is, it could be argued, in the art which matters, especially by women.

At St Martin's, Gallagher studied sculpture as well as painting and drawing, not photography, and was subsequently self-taught in filmmaking. Her sculptural background is retained in the sense of each film being a unique object, with its own texture. There is also a biographical suspicion that she lives and works in relative isolation from the established art world, choosing to protect herself from the standardisation of commercial and critical pressures. The result is a wonderfully individualistic body of work, little like anything by anybody else of Gallagher's generation. Often even the subjects of her films, whether people or animals, have separated themselves from society. One example of this characteristic is Animalation, in which the camera is focused, close-up, for the whole duration of the film on a saola, a rare species of antelope found only in the Annamite Mountain Range on the border between Vietnam and Laos. Gallagher had been seeking an opportunity to film a saola for several years, eventually doing so after an intrepid trek following

112

her look-out's tip-off. The mahogany-brown animal, with long, striped, sharply pointed horns, appears to be asleep in a jungle glade. A butterfly lands on its back. Three or four flies buzz around the moist nostrils. Nothing much else happens. The light changes as wind blows branches across the sun's angled rays. There is no soundtrack; the film is entirely silent. The saola may be dead.

By a curious paradox typical of Gallagher's oeuvre, sound is in fact a central feature in most of her other films, merging into the overtly musical even when derived from documentary-type recordings. The soundtracks of several of her movies are drawn directly from her live musical experiences, including regular attendance at avant-garde concerts in London. Well versed in the classics of contemporary music, works by Stockhausen, Feldman, Xenakis and the rest, she also attends improvised music performances at Café Oto, a short walk from her home in North London. She greatly admires the saxophone playing of Evan Parker; at least three of her soundtracks are influenced by his perfection of the technique of circular breathing, which enables him to produce an un-broken sound from his instrument for a full forty minutes. Gallagher also commissions composer/musicians to contribute new music to her soundtracks, including the percussionist Julian Broadhurst and the young sitar star Anoushka Shankar.

About *May Tomorrow Shine the Brightest Of All Your Many Days As It Will Be Your Last*, one of the films due to be shown at Camden Arts Centre, Gallagher says: 'The soundtrack is cobbled together from Dictaphone record-ings, old 78s, hisses, scratches and whines. The title is taken from Borges; it's a letter one king writes to another, the evening before they go into battle.'

Gallagher was given her first photographic camera

on her tenth birthday, described by her as 'a present of ingratiation' from her mother's then-partner. She was instantly obsessed by the taking of still photographs, until the making of moving images came to dominate her life soon after the end of her time at St Martin's, through loan by the school of a Bolex H16. At the group show *Time Signed* at the ICA in 2001, Gallagher declined to exhibit any film, and instead mounted six different classic Bolex cameras on sculpture plinths. Occasionally she has her 16mm film telecined and then edits digitally on screen before reconverting the final article to film, whilst asserting her preference wherever possible for hand-processing from start to finish.

Solomon Anstrader

[In consultation with me, three stills from my work were chosen to illustrate this brochure and two reference images proposed by the writer, an art historian currently based in Berlin. As usual at Camden Arts Centre, the essay was written before the contents of the show were finalised, the booklet designed and printed to be available in advance of the opening.]

—

Dear Lynn
Found myself more interested in your exhibition leaflet than I expected. Genuinely.
What a strange way of thinking you have. Pulled it off, though, it seems.
Good for you.
Can see the CAC is a smart place to be.
I'm pleased for myself as well as for you.
Kisses, Mother xxx

Mother
Comments appreciated. Would you like to come down
to see it? You could stay with us in Dalston for a few
days, we've plenty of room.
It's on for another two and half months, so no hurry. Let
me know what suits.
Love
L

[Though not particularly appropriate, on this card I
painted out in modernist blocks of blue, pink and yellow the figure of the Duke of Edinburgh in a colour
postcard of Sandringham House, leaving the Queen
standing alone in her cream cardigan, below-the-knee
tweed skirt and dark green woollen stockings, the lake
and house behind her. No dogs.]

—

L
What about 9th to 16th of May?
M x

[Post Office postcard.]

29 APR 03

Mother
Fixed! In the book!
Let me know the arrival time of your train and I'll meet
you at Euston.
Seventeen years since we last saw each other!

Why?

My decision to stay away, I don't deny. Intentional, not by mistake.

You bear some responsibility too, Mum. 'It takes two to tango' you used to say, too often, because you knew how much the phrase annoyed me. 'We are NOT tangoing! I don't actually know what a tango is. Some kind of sexy dance? You'll've done plenty of that!' I remember shouting. Something of the same. When I was about twelve.

It was the men, basically. All your men. Spongers. And drunks.

The worst was when I quite liked them. Let them touch me up. It was horrible.

You must have been as happy to get rid of me as I was to go. Stop the teenage lush interfering with your bloody men!

Nothing to be ashamed of. Loads of mothers and daughters can't stand the sight of each other. I decided not to pretend.

Not pretending now, either. Things are OK, finally.

Have you changed a lot? In the flesh, I mean. Photos deceive.

I have. On the platform, look out for a woman with very short peroxide blonde hair and a double chin!

Till soon

Love

Lynn

—

Dear Lynn

Before we meet, I need to tell you something.

Though you haven't seen me for many years, I've seen you. The last time quite recently, at Camden Arts Centre. So I know you've a peroxide crew-cut these days. And that you don't have any kind of double chin!

I've come to almost all your openings, as a matter of fact. Starting with the degree show at St Martin's. I was so fed up with your refusal to come up to see me, I decided to come down. Incognito, as they say. In a reddish wig and sunglasses. Not as flash as it sounds. Dressed ordinary.

Worn the same kind of get-up ever since. Surprised you didn't notice a regular not-so-young lady in the crowd? Not that you were always at the openings. Did see you at the Susan Hiller preview in Davies Street. She's terrific, I agree.

There were times when I was so fed up with you that I nearly didn't turn up. Like your first show at Mansfield Art. Can't remember now what that particular row was about. Knowing that you wouldn't spot me, I came, though, and am glad I did. Was moved by those strange mouth photos you made. Not sure why, exactly. Actually, you weren't there anyway!

After a while, other regulars started to recognise me and chat as if I was part of the scene. Without knowing who I was. Without caring.

Sad place, the art world.

Had to stop myself going over to you now and again. To cheer you up. Could see you were hating it.

I used to stay longer than you ever did, looking at the work. I liked it all. Well, admired it all, anyway. And completely loved **Sea Change Scene***. That was quite something, really. I can't imagine how you've turned out to be someone able to make something like that. So completely beautiful.*

All gone now, that one? Except for record photos.

I so much hope that you'll still want me to come and stay in your house on the 9th.

With love

Mother

[On receiving this letter from Mum, I telephoned her, our correspondence resuming when she returned home to Sparkhill from her visit to me]

—

Dear Lynn
Wanted to say that I'm proud of my daughter. To a degree.
Owning a decent house in a more-or-less central part of London,
that's an achievement. Before you're forty.
Thanks very much for having me to stay.
XX

[Mother wrote this on an American commercial post-card of a night attack on Baghdad, bombs exploding, buildings falling, the sky red the explosions yellow, re-flected in the River Tigris.]

28 MAY 03

Thanks, Mum, I'm glad you had an OK time with us.
I've followed your advice about keeping – getting! – fit.
Bought jogging gear and established a three-times-a-week route.
Speed walk over to Hackney Downs and jog three or four times around the perimeter, beneath the trees, try-ing to see into the houses beyond the railings.
Feel worse not better!
It'll improve.
With love
Lynn

[On the portrait postcard of a grim-looking Vito Acconci, one of my favourite artists, taken at the age of nineteen in 1959 on national service in the U.S. Marine Platoon Leader Corps, dressed in military fatigues and holding a rifle.]

13 JUNE 03

Mother
Went the other night to a concert you'd have liked. Acid Brass by a nattily alternative artist I know called Jeremy Deller. He persuaded the traditional Williams Fairey Brass Band to play at the QEH a repertoire he'd devised of acid house music!
Lynn XX

P.S. Only just noticed: Lynn/linnet. I'm a songbird!

[One of several of these marquetry-type cards that I have made, giving them titles on the backs. This I called *Her Favourite Subject*, the careful cutting out from a colour postcard of the full-length standing photo of young Queen Elizabeth at her coronation and cutting her in beside a black and white early studio portrait postcard of an ordinary young man. The visiting card type postcard of 1905 I remember buying from Camden Market, back in the eighties.]

—

Lynn
I can read, you know.
You've twice asked where I stayed on my visits to your previews. Didn't reply because you only ever write about things connected to yourself.
What about me separate from you? Have you a clue what it is I

care about, for myself? No, and don't give a monkey's. You're as self-centred as you've always been.

In point of fact, I used to stay the night in a dirt-cheap hotel near King Cross Station. Doss house, really. Breakfast at a great little café, Mario's. Lovely bloke. Into music. Then walk up the road to catch the train from Euston back to Birmingham. Satisfied?

Mother

29 SEPT 03

Mother

You've got me wrong. I don't dislike individual people. It's 'people' I can't stand, the in-crowd, slinking around at private views, eyes on stalks for someone more important to talk to.

I've agreed to do a show at Hauser & Wirth in Zurich to prove to them all that I could.

I wish I hadn't.

Lesson learnt.

Bridget said it would be 'good for my career' and I was too surprised by the remark to pull her up. It was arranged in a jiffy, wham, bam, thank you ma'am.

I did sort-of like the idea of H & W's old brewery on the banks of the river in Zurich. Even though I know they only asked me because of the Camden accolades. Not for my work itself.

Enough. Their money-talk turns my stomach. I'll look better after myself in future.

The press release is junk, jargon, an insult. Interchangeable with hundreds of thousands of others. Middle-man pollution.

You did ask, Mum! Now you know!

Lynn xx

P.S. I threw away the press release – here's the translation Bridget has had made of the review in *Das Kunstmagazin*, which I'm pleased with.

Photographs & Film
New work by Lynn Gallagher
September 25 to October 22, 2003
Mon to Fri 11.00–6.00. Sat 11.00–5.00
Hauser & Wirth, Limmatstrasse 270,
8005 Zürich

This is a more intimate exhibition than we have come to expect of Hauser & Wirth, a limited number of works of small scale: two sets of photographs and a black-and-white film twenty minutes in length. It is a relief to step away from the grandiose high fashion of the art recently shown in their converted Löwenbräu Brewery and relish the quiet beauty and palpable sincerity of this young – not yet forty – British artist Lynn Gallagher.

The first group of photographs are the unposed portrait heads of people, both men and women and of all ages, with radically different coloured eyes, which the artist describes as 'a rare condition called chimerism, which is caused by the fusion of two fertilized eggs (non-identical twins) at a very early stage of gestation in the womb.' I imagine that Gallagher took some time tracking down these telling subjects.

The other photographic series, *The Lost Room,* mounts together the black-and-white photographs she took of the room in which she briefly stayed in Paraguay, paired with the pinky-red circular images derived from her remarkable mouth pictures. In the room photos, Gallagher recorded details which she believed would be erased by time from her memory, quotidian things

121

such as how a table leg met the floor and the profile of a skirting board.

The sense of actual and impending loss in the room of photographs is echoed by the film *There Is A Happy Land Further Awaay,* also situated in foreign lands, in this instance on the Pacific archipelago of Vanuatu. As visible in the film, it was Gallagher's wish to visit somewhere wholly unknown to her, with no familiar sights to trigger existing aesthetic responses. The film is over-voiced by a friend of hers reading Henri Michaux's poem 'I am writing to you from a far-off country', the mistakes and repetitions retained as symbol of the poem's, and the film's, descriptions of a distant land which is ultimately ungraspable.

Helmut Bovier

—

Dear Lynn
Isn't that Olafur Eliasson a genius? Saw a programme on him on the telly. The Turbine Hall looked amazing, with hundreds of people lying on the ground.
Not you, I don't imagine!
XX

[Written by Mum on a free tear-off postcard from the West Midlands Safari Park in Kidderminster, of giraffes towering above a red Mini.]

23 NOV 03

Mother
Eliasson is a showman, an elephant trainer. Technological trickery to develop, enormous amounts of money to

122

mount, and monumental self-importance to promote. I tell you, I loathe men with his arrogance.

Gormley's as bad. Have you heard the biblical tone of his banal pronouncements on the radio recently? Forty years making models of himself. As if he's God's cousin. The only thing of his I like is the early bread piece, preserved in wax, the outline of his body lying on a double mattress beside the silhouette of his wife.

Sir 'Antony' Gormley. Couldn't be an Anthony, could he? Not special enough. Bet he changed the spelling himself.

Angel of the North is, for sure, a monumental triumph of popularity. Fine, if that's what you're after.

As for Kapoor, he's ... I'm lost for words. So pretentious. In person and the work. And that's being charitable!

Ah, well!

Hold your nerve and sidestep the pundits, I say.

Say to myself, that is. Not to you, you're fine as you are. You're my Mum!

With love

Lynn

—

Dear Lynn

I don't know what you'd suggest I could do but I've been having for some time now terrible nightmares. At least I think they're terrible. Maybe it's normal?

I wake up before meeting my fate. The worst thing is that the demons don't disappear, they remain in my bedroom. Turn the light on, open my eyes, and there they still are. As if they really existed. I'm completely terrified.

I may tend to drink a touch too much serving in the pub. Difficult to resist the free offers from men.

Not good for me, I know, but doesn't explain how those awful
pictures appear in my head.
Where do they come from?
What can I do?
Sorry to bother you.
Love
Mother

19 DEC 03

Dear Mother

Sounds dreadful.

I don't know what to say.

Everyone dreams, and it's generally accepted that the process is essentially restorative, that subconscious night-thinking is one of the protective methods open to all of us to help deal with our unpalatable imaginings. Might it be less frightening if you accepted that the demons are of your own making, rather than infernal creatures attacking from outside?

If the nightmares continue, why don't you take time off and come and stay with us for a week or two?

You could tell us at breakfast each morning what happened to you during the night.

It helps to talk. Richard's a much better listener than I am.

Drink won't be a temptation as we both gave up alcohol on January 1st 2000. Haven't touched a drop since. Haven't wanted to.

Come at the end of the month, stay as long as you like.

With love

Lynn xx

—

Thanks, love, hearing from you helps in itself.
I'll be all right.
Can't afford to miss all the overtime over the holidays.
Don't worry, I'll be fine.
Love
Mum

P.S. When I do next come down I'd like to see your studio.

[This was sent on a peculiar postcard, for Mum, published in Leicester by the National Association of Youth Clubs, the black-and-white snap of a group of teenage boys in the street with the caption across the top, printed as if hand-written: *'Why is it us girls are kept in, when it's the boys who cause the trouble?'*]

28 DEC 03

M
DO look after yourself.
XLX

[I raided my store of 1980s postcards by the activist Bunch of Artists, this one of a behatted Mrs Thatcher photo-montaged to face a large Dalmatian dog, with the caption *SPOTTED BITCH!!*]

8 JAN 04

M
As it's you, I'll let you visit the studio. Normally I don't allow anyone in, not even Bridget. Definitely no journalists. Just an assistant, when I have one. And Richard, of course. And my friend Lindsay.

They're the only people to whom I've told the address. Apart from carriers, collecting and delivering work or materials.

It's because I need to know that what I do in the studio, who I am at my work, and how and where things are going is for me to deal with, nobody else.

There's no doorbell.

The studio is on two floors. You'll find that the ground floor, where I spend most of my time, looks more like a lab than the conventional idea of an artist's studio. There's masses of equipment, some of it pretty sophisticated, developers and cameras and printers and lights and screens. Recording equipment. And the rest. The top room is kept completely bare, ready for set-up shoots. White blinds on all the windows.

There's a loo, and a mini kitchen.

What else can I tell you?

Come and see, sometime.

L xx

14 JAN 04

Mother

I'll be travelling a lot this coming year, to make two new films. And exhibitions abroad, here and there. It's disruptive and anxious-making. I'd like Richard to be with me, at least some of the time, but his work is insanely time-consuming. Anyway, he has a pathological fear of flying.

There we are.

Hope 2004 brings you some good things.

Lots of love

Lynn

—

Dear Lynn
I've had a bit of an accident. Nothing serious
I was walking home from work at the pub and tripped, twisted my ankle on the curb. So painful that I couldn't get up, lay there half on the pavement, tights torn, knee bleeding. Passers-by were helping me, when a young policewoman stuck her nose in. You know the type, shiny hair tied back in a dinky cap. Jolly voice. I told her what had happened and she said: 'Oh! Bless you.'
Can't tell you how much I dislike the way fit young women address doddery old things like me.
I replied, loudly: 'I'm an atheist.'
I'm not, actually. I'm a Jew, in spirit.
Mother xx

P.S. Notice that your last postcard was published in Dublin. James Joyce and all that. See, I'm not a total write-off!

03 FEB 04

You tell them, Mum!
xxx me

[Sent a local postcard bought in the paper shop at Dalston Kingston Station, of the street market on Ridley Road, a wet-fish stall in the foreground.]

127

Mother
You won't be pleased to hear this.
I've refused to be shortlisted for the Turner Prize this year. The invitation, weeks before the public announcement, presumes agreement and my 'no' rocked them back on their stiletto heels. No deal, despite thinly veiled threats over the telephone from the panel Chair.
I'm dead against celebrity-making of artists. Against in general the divisive listing of winners and losers. Prizes one side and zilch the other.
Best bloody British!
Jesus! It's crystal clear. Painters, filmmakers, sculptors, whatever, we compete against ourselves not each other. So obvious that I'm embarrassed writing it.
You won't understand my Turner turn-down.
Understanding is overrated, anyhow!
My guts tied themselves in a knot as I read the letter and I decided then and there to say no. Bridget was supportive. While warning that the art world will take against me for dishing the system.
Let them.
We'll see, we'll see.
I will see!
Love from
Lynn

—

Dear Lynn
I think you're mad, but don't take any notice of me, love.
Do what suits you. You've made many more better decisions in your life than I have in mine.

Stick to your guns, I say.
Mother xx

[Written on a postcard of Millais' *The Blind Girl*, one of the Pre-Raphaelite paintings in the collection of Birmingham Museum & Art Gallery. Mum may have remembered how jealous I used to be of the girl's red hair.]

8 MAR 04

Thanks, Mum! I like the Yiddisher my-child-can-do-no-wrong line!
Coincidentally, I've been reading a recently published book by an American academic called Ruth Klüger. After years and years of silence, in this book, *Landscapes of Memory*, she writes of her and her mother's deportation from Vienna, in 1942, when she was only eleven, and of their survival, somehow, through the death camps.
Klüger actually says: 'When I ask myself today how and why an unbeliever like me can call herself a Jew, one of several possible answers runs: "It's because of Theresienstadt. That is where I became a Jew".'
Her restraint is so moving.
Must remember that in my work.
I do, mostly.
L XX

—

Dear Lynn
Since you fancy me as a pretend Jewish mother, I've a kvetch question to ask. What have you got against kids?
You've been like that since you were small.

I can't recall you ever playing properly with your cousins,
Betty's two. And you've never wanted children of your own.
Why?
A question, not a criticism.
Love
Mother

22 MAR 04

Mother

Don't ask me.

Why's the sky blue?

God knows.

No, God does NOT know. Because HE is a figment of the imagination, the invention of authority.

One of the few things I do know is that God is the creation of man and not the other way round ... On second thoughts, women were pretty early into god-creating too, so I can't blame men alone.

As a matter of fact, there's at least one child I like a lot. Sarah S.'s daughter Evlyn, a totally terrific little girl, with a murderous vocabulary, double dimples, and personal style in dress – costume, really.

I remember the day I stopped for a chat with Sarah in Curtain Road and she told me she was pregnant, worried about the pressure of parenthood on her work as an artist. Essentially happy, though, to be becoming a mum. This happiness has cloaked her little girl, kept her feeling safe. Protected Evlyn's specialness.

Love

Lynn

P.S. In case it doesn't show, and in case I haven't properly told you before: I'm so pleased knowing that you came

to see my exhibitions all those times, without telling me.
Everything is different now.

—

Dear Lynn
You learnt the no-God stuff from me. Don't you remember?
I can understand why people invented a God.
Or Gods, doesn't matter.
Easier to believe there's someone in control. That some genius
sees meaning behind the nonsense of human life.
Enough. No need for me to go on about it.
Glad to see you got the message loud and clear.
Atheists unite!
Love, Mother

12 JULY 04

Mother
Weird! I think my father must have registered me as
next of kin.
Because I've received an official letter from the Foreign
and Commonwealth Office notifying me of his death, in
jail. Malaga, this time. Shot point-blank in the temple.
By another prisoner, they presume. Nobody expects to
find out for certain who it was.
Why should they bother?
Won't have done it to himself, the selfish sod.
They're holding a bit of personal stuff to send on to me.
The FCO enclosed three official-looking letters to sign.
In Spanish, which I can't read. Will get them translated.
Don't worry, I won't bother you with any more of this,
just thought you should know that he's gone.
With love, Lynn

Mother

Can't you start to write to me again? Has mention of Dad silenced you? Let's not give him the power, please. Anyway ... Always 'anyway'. Bad habit. A tic ... Anyhow ... Anyroads ... Ugh!

The art world's gearing up again after the summer break. Susan is back from Florida and I called for a catch-up tea. With a present for her, a beautiful little book newly published by an artist still in his twenties, Ryan Gander, titled *The Boy Who Always Looked Up*. The main character is a boy called Tom, who lives with his mum in a fictional version of Ernö Goldfinger's Trellick Tower, which I pass close to in the train a couple of minutes out of Paddington Station on the way West.

Goldfinger appears as himself in the book, which concludes with a conversation between the architect and the boy on the roof of the building:

'Why do you look up, Tom?' he asked, pushing his small round spectacles back up his nose.

'I think it's because it seems better up there than down there,' he said, wiping his nose on the sleeve of his jumper. 'Because it's empty up here in the sky, and when I look up I feel like I can do anything, like anything's possible.'

Ernö smiled back at him.

'Now don't be sad, Tom. Do you know what grown-ups call that?' he said.

'No,' Tom said, shaking his head wildly and wiping the tears from his cheeks, which were now streaming from his eyes.

'Aspiration,' he replied

I thought of Susan for this book because of the modernist

estate around the corner from her studio, where construction began the year Goldfinger's Trellick Tower was completed. Beautiful rarities, both buildings. In Britain, that is. Common on the Continent.

I bet Gander comes from a ridiculously happy family, with loyal, non-golfing, socialist, hetero parents!

Susan told me she's signed up with a smart Mayfair dealer, Timothy Taylor. Not for the money. For museums. For Taylor to place her stuff in public collections.

Her first show begins there in the spring, *The J Street Project*, which she's been working on for three years, chasing down all the streets and alleyways in Germany which still bear the word 'Jude'. Ended up with photographs and information on three hundred and three sites, documented in still images, video, and a book

I'm not sure about Taylor.

Inaccurate.

I *am* sure about him. Sure that I despise the place people like him occupy in the art world, peddling West End privilege and prestige. To clients with gigantically too much money and nil conscience.

I'm afraid Susan will hate being part of the Taylor entourage, hate them speaking for her: the misrepresentations, the currency deals, the flattery and fiddles. The smooth-talking hypocrisy.

She'll survive. If any living artist has the strength to skittle the establishment it's Susan Hiller!

With love

from

Lynn xx

—

Dear Lynn
I've been thinking. Isn't it high time you learnt to drive?
I know getting knocked off your bike that time set you back.
You went on about the driver, a nurse on the way to work, how
terrible she must have felt. Swore you never ever wanted to put
yourself in her position.
That's years ago now. You need to be able to drive. For your
work. To get to out-of-the-way places for filming.
Nobody's going to make you bash into bicyclists!
You're so pig-headed. Why cut off your nose to spite your face?
Mother x

22 OCT 04

Mother
For the umpteenth time: I have no desire to drive a car.
Lynn

[A perfect card for the occasion. One of Jacky Fleming's
postcards of her tousle-haired little girl with red bow
and fierce frown, writing on the blackboard: *yes means*
YES and no means NO ... I expect you'll want that repeating.]

21 JAN 05

Mother
You're odd, like me. About shopping, for instance.
Both of us put off buying things for as long as we can.
Especially clothes.
Yesterday I couldn't delay any more the purchase of a
new batch of lightweight shirts and trousers, sweaters
and windcheaters and things for my travels, the old ones
in tatters. To save time, I always go to the same shop,
Rohan in Covent Garden. Though not cheap, their

clothes are great for me, in pastel greys and browns. Dry in an hour from sudden rain, or after washing overnight on the trail.

Why am I telling you this? Such a bore, your daughter! What is interesting, I think, is that from Rohan I walked up to Endell Street for fish and chips and a mug of tea at The Rock & Sole Plaice. And the walls were covered in postcards! Stuck to the white tiles in patterned blocks of beetles and shells and shoes and pop stars and men at work and the Lake District and pub signs and fruit.

A kind of artwork. Tasty.

The food too!

Then on to the Barbican for Théâtre de Complicité's new show, *The Elephant Vanishes*. Somewhat confusing as the company is English, run by Simon McBurney, who is the son of an American archaeologist, presenting a play adapted from three Murakami short stories, performed in Japanese by an all-Japanese cast, with endless technical invention.

I loved every moment.

Video screens whizzed across the stage, projecting images which imitate cars and trains without looking or sounding quite like them. Actors relax on vertical beds over which the sleeper's other self hovers like a restless angel.

That's theatre!

With love

Lynn

4 AUG 05

Dear Mother

Wanted to thank you for staying calm when we packed up your flat last week.

It was pretty traumatic, for me, returning to Sparkhill after so long. At least you'd moved from our house, saving me those sights. Though I did recognise your new street. Was it Pete and Jenny who lived there?

Very little in general has changed about the place. Dingier. It's good you've gone to the Costa Brava.

Are things OK?

I admire your realism. You never hope for too much.

You were well prepared, with your list of tasks, the furniture labelled, plenty of cardboard boxes and packing paper. It's from you that I must have inherited my mania for order.

I'm glad too that you'd kept some of my children's books in the move to the flat from home. They feel right here now in Dalston. Interesting how they were considered boys books at the time.

Tarka the Otter was both, I suppose. And the girl in *Swallows and Amazons* has always been seen as the boss, essentially.

Gender confusion? Gender war? Gender indifference? When I went down to St Martin's, didn't I leave in my room dozens of pop records? Not knowing at the time that I'd never be back. When, I wonder, did you clear my bedroom? To rent to one of your men?

Never mind.

Thanks Mum, you're a brick.

L XXX

—

Dear Lynn

I meant to say, there's no point trying to make me stop dyeing my hair black. You may think it looks 'false', I don't care, I like it. Going to the hairdresser is one of the few pleasures left to a single woman of my age. Especially in Spain.

While I remember: I've put my mother's amethyst brooch in the back of the cutlery drawer here in my kitchenette, for safe keeping. I know you'll never wear it. Never have myself. Not my taste. Or shall I give it to Betty? She liked Mum. God knows how.

I think I'm going to be all right here. The sun eats up the day. Gone before it begins. Time flies by.

Love
Mother

3 SEPT 05

Mother

Shifting things around in the house the other day, I found the corpse of a mouse in a large empty vase.

Poor thing, probably jumped in to escape Absalom. Months ago, it must have been. The dried body odourless, feather-light.

Slightly surprised Abbie didn't knock the vase over to get at the mouse!

You asked why I've never put cats in a film. I think it's because I know too much about them. Anyway, who wants more soppy pics of cats.

On what floor is your flat? Is the view OK?

Love

Lynn

20 OCT 05

You're a Peter Sellers fan aren't you, Mum?

Saw at the BFI this week a restored print of *Dr Strangelove*. Sellers so funny and clever in all three of his parts. 1964 it was made and still feels radical. The time for change sure is overdue!

Little DOES change.

Too easy to bury unpleasant truths and totter along in the usual way.

Love, me

[This card was made by Leeds Postcards for CND, printed on a black ground with the sky-blue words, in sloping letters: *Clouseau fans against the beumb*, referring to another of Peter Sellers' classic roles.]

18 JAN 06

Mother

I have never started a conversation with anyone on the tube. Nobody. Ever.

With one exception. Yesterday!

On the Northern Line between Euston and Waterloo the pale dark-haired girl sitting beside me was reading my Camden Arts Centre brochure!

And I couldn't resist introducing myself. She blushed. So did I.

Lovely girl, graduated last summer from Wimbledon College of Art. She's Portuguese, a nurse by profession, who paid her way first to England and then through art school by night-watching rich old private patients.

Anna-Clara's her name.

I wonder how her work looks? Nothing like mine, she assured me. The stitching and painting of canvas collages, I think she said.

'I'm sorry I didn't catch your show,' she told me, shortly before leaving the train. 'At least I have the catalogue.'

Quite something to happen.

With love, Lynn

Dear Lynn

How's gay Richard, still around?

You say he isn't but I guarantee he is, basically. Hollow-chested. Winks. Unless he's got eye problems. Which wouldn't be great for an artist. Won't be content to live off your success forever. I warn you. Not without punishing you somehow.

Explains why you don't have a baby, him being gay.

That café the two of you go to down the road, Tina We Salute You, that's a gay haunt, you can tell. The paintings of nude women look like men with boobs. Sweet dark boys from Brazil cooking cupcakes in the kitchen.

He's helped you make a nice home, I grant you. Eye for colour. Unless that's you?

Four floors, for two people and two cats. Ridley Market round the corner and that delicious Turkish restaurant a short walk. Not bad.

Mind you, what would I know, you've only let me visit once.

I'm lonely. Very.

What's the point?

Mother

20 MAR 06

Mother

Don't suppose you keep a copy of your letters to me.

A pity. Because if you reread your last one, I reckon not even you could fail to see how self-indulgent you are. Emotionally ill-disciplined, to put it mildly.

Speaking to me like that, as you have done off and on since I was a child, no longer hurts. In fact, it's quite helpful, because it's so blatantly wrong and therefore reassures me, finally, after years of guilt and doubt, that I

139

was right to leave home, right to cut free from you, right to keep you at a distance.

When I was a teenager your mood swings terrified me, they came without warning or explanation. I'm shaking my head at my desk. Because I know you'll have no idea what I'm trying to say. And that's why. Why I didn't want to see you. Won't any longer tear the quick of my fingers to shreds, hurl my bag against the bedroom door. Against your selfishness.

A particular incident, which happened to me here in London, about six years after I left art school, has helped me take better care of myself in this respect. A friend, sort of friend, colleague let's say, had had a baby by another young artist. The two have remained together ever since, a proper couple. She was troubled, though, quite troublingly troubled, still is confused in her head, about almost everything. From the window of the small studio I shared then in Wapping, I saw this girl – with a pushchair in which sat, strapped tight, her two-year-old son – stop by the warehouse wall in the narrow street and bash her forehead repeatedly against the bricks, screaming. There was blood and tears. She walked on pushing her child down the pavement.

What an earth could this have meant to him?

He must have been frightened. I certainly was, watching from above.

To me it meant: stay away from your mother.

Sorry, I shouldn't be writing this to you.

Sorry.

Love

Lynn

—

Lynn
It's so irritating that you won't have a mobile phone, to text and chat. You being difficult, as per usual. Eccentric, Betty used to say, to be polite. Bloody-minded spite more like.
And Skype? Why won't you sign us up for Skype? You could Skype me in Spain.
Don't tell me. You value your privacy.
I'm your MOTHER!

[Written on a Spanish-published postcard of the pin-up Bettie Page photographed on a beach, captioned in large red and yellow sloping letters: *Fun In The Sun*.]

—

Dear Lynn
You've gone silent on me again. Which isn't fair, you're all I've got.
The money comes in, appears in the bank every month as usual, and I'm grateful for that. Money's not everything, though, Money's nothing, in the end. 'Can't buy me love, love, money can't buy me lo-o-ove'. Great song. Came out the year before you were born, as far as I remember. Those were the days.
Good calamares and papas fritas here. Different from Margate. Better, now I'm used to them.
Much better. No comparison, really.
I wish you'd write.
Love
Mother

—

Dear Lynn
How long are you going to keep this up?

Silence is a form of torture, according to the Geneva Convention.
It said so on British TV last night.
You're impossible, you really are.
Love, all the same
Mother

[Sent on the publicity postcard from a Spanish vine-yard, the colour photo of two bronzed couples drinking wine at either side of a rustic table, beneath overhanging ruby grapes.]

03 JUNE 06

Mother

Would you please try see things from my point of view? You don't have to agree, you simply have to try and accept that it's how I feel.

Of course this isn't at all 'simple', that's a silly thing for me to write. It may be that it's impossible for a mother to tolerate a daughter's differences. Especially when as fundamental as me with you.

One more good reason for me not to have a child. What kind of monster might I give birth to, blood-related to us two!

Mobile phone. OK, I'll have another go at explaining. I don't have a mobile phone in order to be free, so nobody can presume right of access to me.

I can't be got at, disturbed, distracted, made to feel guilty for not replying.

Side benefits: not getting knocked down by a car when absent-mindedly checking messages while crossing the road; look at art rather than photograph it; read on the tube instead of playing stupid games; no last-minute change of arrangements for meeting a friend for tea.

Doesn't bother me if people don't turn up, I read, have lunch or whatever and get on with my day.

And I don't want to feel you in my pocket, jabbing me in the ribs!

Will that do you?

The sort of silence which I abhor is the withholding of information which people have a right to know: like why a father abandoned his daughter before she was three!

Love

Lynn

13 JUNE 06

Mum

What fun! You've gone silent now!

Lynn xxx

[One of the few things I remember hearing about my father at the time was that he had once been in the merchant navy, 'sailing the high seas' as Mum put it. With the result that ships and freight have periodically attracted me. On this 1970s postcard, titled on the reverse *Sea Trips, Wells*, I painted in acrylic onto the bows of two beached fishing boats a red and a green rectangular steel shipping container.]

—

Dear Lynn

Everyone has secrets, hides things dangerous to reveal.

I think the American tell-all talk which came in after the war is rubbish, worse than us po-faced British. In the fifties, when I was a teenager, there were American airmen all over the place, flush with money and themselves and I detested it. There was

my dad, working his butt off for them in the repair shed at
Mildenhall Airbase, and they swanned around town happy as
Larry, patting young girls on the bum.
And more.
Who could I tell?
No one except Dad. Who I knew couldn't afford to believe me.
So didn't bother, kept it to myself.
You knuckle down, bury your own shit.
Truth is it never bothered me.
Telling is overdone, big time. Give it a rest about silence, love,
please. We've both got better things to think about.
Your cats. How're the cats? Has the big ginger's paw healed?
That time I visited he sat on my lap when you were off working
in your studio. Lovely cat. Shy. Undemanding.
Let's try to be friends.
Your mother

19 JUNE 06

Mother

You can't hide forever.

By now it doesn't matter to me. You're the one who suffers. Why do you imagine every man you've ever slept with has done the dirty? Disappeared without trace at the first opportunity?

Except the parasites, that is. The leeches.

Because they discover that you don't exist, that behind the sexy make-up is a mask. A blank. Nothing.

It's never too late, people say. In your case, I'm not so sure.

I'm sad for you.

Your daughter xx

[On this National Gallery postcard, *Portrait of a Woman*

by Robert Campin. I had scraped the surface away to white undercard, leaving only the cream cloth headgear. A no-person. Empty. I prefer to open-send postcards, stamped and addressed on the back, but this card I did post in an envelope, to avoid damage, and to allow my writing to spread over onto the address side. Glad she kept it, pleased to have it back.]

27 JUNE 06

Mother
I've stopped jogging.
Caught sight of myself the other day reflected in a shop window, red in the face, lycra-tight crotch and bum.
No, Sir!
Such a relief!
Love
Lynn

[Wrote this on the back of a unique postcard by the mail-artist Anna Banana, which I must have bought sometime on eBay, signed and dated by her October 1979, collaging a giant yellow banana into the arms of a postcard starlet, adding the triple speech bubbles: *I like bananas   because they have no bones!*]

28 SEPT 06

Dear Mother
I've decided that you influenced my artistic taste rather more than I'd imagined.
Seriously.
I'll never forget the way you became a different person on our visits to the Playhouse pantomime when I was

young. You laughed and laughed. Threw your arms around, sang along, shouted. I loved you being so alive, and extra-adored the performances for doing this to you. Didn't last. Back to normal by the time we reached home on the bus.

This brief annual sight of how you could be was heart-breaking. Literally.

What I wanted to say is that some of the art-videos which I like best today sort of meld with those joyful evenings back then.

My favourite at the moment is *Sleeper*, by a Londoner, Mark Wallinger.

Dressed head-to-toe in a realistic bear costume, he was videoed spending nine consecutive nights locked behind the plate glass foyer walls of the Neue Nationalgalerie in Berlin. Wandering around in bewilderment, pressing himself up against the glass to inveigle visitors, and lying flat out on the hall floor to rest. Towards the end of his run of nightly performances a stranger turned up outside dressed in an identical brown bear costume. To Wallinger's surprise and evident glee, they pranced around together either side of the glass.

It's not *Puss in Boots*, I know. It is pantomime, though. Don't you think? Maybe you'd have to see it to say.

People call this kind of thing 'videoed performance art', whereas I make film. I do love the directness, though, of video.

Ah well!

Love, Lynn

P.S. I'm always afraid that the images I create are too fragile to be noticed. My still photos as well as the films. Afraid they'll fall unseen through cracks in the floorboards.

Mum

Richard knows Gilbert & George.

Know who I mean?

You must know. The couple who go around in tweedy-type buttoned suits and eat every meal out, breakfast included, because they don't have a kitchen. Because they don't want to waste art-time with shopping or dishes.

They often have dinner at that Turkish restaurant you like. Richard joins them there from time to time. As a student he used to work for G & G in their Spitalfields studio, assembling the big photo pieces.

They've just sent him an invitation to a special dinner after the private view next month of their Tate Modern show, with SWALK written in large letters in black ink across the back of the envelope.

Sealed With A Loving Kiss! SWALK! That's your era, isn't it? Teenage bopping at the base?

G & G's best piece of work, I think, is their partnership itself. Seamless since falling in love at St Martin's in 1967. Chink-less. The perfect marriage.

They own two houses in Fournier Street, with an Indian family in the building in between. I suggested to Richard he persuade them to live one in each, to protect the relationship from over-familiarity.

Richard looked worried, unsure what might lie behind my remark.

Actually, we're getting married in the spring. Largely because I want him to have full legal control over my films should anything happen to me.

Have you made a will? Do you want me to be executor?

Lynn XXX

—

Dear Lynn

Of course I've made a will. Not that there'll be anything left worth having by then. The apartment's only rented. A hundred quid's worth of premium bonds. Must find the receipt. Still got the flash watch your dad gave me. Worth a thousand quid he said, back then. Could be, if it was stolen. Which it probably was.

It's all yours. Do what you want with it. And with me.

Don't waste good money on a funeral, or grave. Chuck my ashes into the sea.

Don't fret, I can't swim!

Love

M X

18 FEB 07

Mother

I'm not getting at you. It's just that I'll need to know for probate and things. Eventually. So could you tell me what your tax position is? And pension deal?

You've never had any spending money and I don't begrudge you a bit of an easier life now in Spain. Not at all. It's good that I've cash spare to help a bit.

I'm pleased for you.

As pleased as I am for myself, to earn enough to pay a decent dollop of tax. More, in fact, than I need, as I refuse to let the accountant file the legal dodges he recommends. Never even claim all my legitimate expenses. Hate it when I discover that writers whose novels I admire are tax evaders. Punishing themselves with foreign exile in order to avoid British taxes. Graham Greene stuck in his dreary modern flat in Antibes, John Fowles toying with emigration to Gozo.

Where is Gozo?

Sarah S., who has been reading Fowles' *Journals*, told me of his endless fussing and frothing about the tax demands on his US publication fees and film rights.

How much money do they imagine they need?

Rich, richer, richest ... !

People, they're a lost cause!

With love, Lynn x

—

Dear Lynn

I read something the other day you might like. In a book Betty sent me. The Actual *by Saul Bellow. I'd heard of him but had never considered reading his stuff myself. What do I care about Chicago?*

Not sure why she thought of me for it. Maybe because it's a novel about growing old and about being up for it all the same.

Anyway, I underlined this: 'With me it has been a lifelong principle not to disclose anything to those close to me. Moreover, at any deeper level, what is known is just as inexact and fuzzy as the new information you will presently add to the old.'

Familiar?!

It's quite something for me having time to read and take notes. And think. I used to think of thinking. Sometimes. Not for long. There was never time.

Another life!

Love, Mother

2 MAR 07

Mother

We've got the dates of the wedding. Small and informal.

No church or anything like that. The registry office in Stoke Newington and buffet lunch afterwards at the Turkish place. Tuesday 10th of May.

There'll be more of Richard's family than ours. Many more. He's got two brothers, one in the army, the other a barrister. Or maybe a solicitor?

In Doncaster.

Lawyer, let's say.

The mother died when they were still at secondary school, from peritonitis. Their father didn't marry again, so the four males are close. Plus, Richard's three young nephews now too.

Man overload.

I like his father, he's a decent chap.

You'll meet them all, anyway.

I'm determined to wear nothing special. No hat, nothing fancy. Wasn't even intending to buy a new dress, until Richard suggested I was acting the fanatic. 'Relax,' he said. 'Buy something simple and nice and quietly get though the day. It's for them, not us.' Although I can't stand being told to relax, he has a point.

Wish it was over!

Jesus, I bet someone films it! I'll have to smash their camera!!

With love

Lynn

18 MAY 07

Mother

Who did you see at the wedding?

It's great that you came over.

I saw you talking to Annie, I've known her since St Martin's. She had the cubicle-studio next to mine. And

Lindsay? She was looking forward to meeting you. She's into origins! Can't remember where she's from? The West Country somewhere, I think.

You're back in the sun now. You don't look English anymore, with your colourful long skirts and suntan. Until you speak!

Richard said his dad couldn't work you out!

I'm still catching up with work after the wedding nonsense.

Feeling sad that Sarah S. is moving north to live in Sheffield, unable to afford London any longer. The adorable Evlyn will go too, of course. I admire Sarah, the way she's continued to make politically critical work down the years, despite cold-shouldering by the art establishment. I'm afraid they never forgave her for stepping back from the limelight after *Broken English*.

I'll take the train up to see them one weekend.

Maybe.

Maybe not. I do so hate staying in somebody else's house.

Love

Lynn

—

L

I didn't just come for your wedding. Had family things to sort out, with my cousins in Manchester. It was a good trip.

You looked dishy, and I liked your friend Lindsay. She is bright! Slightly frighteningly so, I must admit. Genuine, though. The real thing.

Being back in England has set me off kilter and I'm having to get used to resort life all over again.

Never mind.

M xxx

P.S. Oh, yes, Gilbert and George came over to say hello at the buffet. George – I think it was, with balding blondish hair? – was ever-so polite, shook my hand and said: 'You're the bride's mother. How do you do. Very important, mothers!'

10 JUNE 07

Mother
Cat report!
The small black one, Absalom, is as tough as anything. I watch him out of the French window at the back, stalking the garden paths, bow-legged, like a prize-fighter. You know he catches rats? Full-size rats almost as big as he is and drags them in through the cat-flap to show us. Up the stairs to me in my bedroom when he's particularly proud of a catch!
At the same time a lap-cat, Abbie is. Spends his evenings curled on my thighs while I'm busy catching up on recorded film.
Happy with cats, better than babies.
Love
Lynn

4 SEPT 08

Mother
Richard and I are on holiday!
Ten days in Devon, renting a coastguard's cottage on the bay at Peppercombe.
It's blissful.
With love
Lynn xx

[I remember that there were no postcards of our secluded

cottage, a rented National Trust property, so I sent Mum this card of boats moored beside the old wharf at nearby Bideford.]

30 SEPT 08

Mother

It was lovely and necessary to spend uninterrupted time alone together, leaving behind in London cameras and things. A pencil and notebook, nothing else. Persuaded Richard, reluctantly, to do the same.

Every morning, while studying over breakfast an Ordnance Survey map of the area, we planned our day's walk. Reckoning on at least three hours and up to seven, if there looked to be a good spot for lunch on route.

Until not long ago, Clovelly must have been enchanting. The tiny harbour still feels genuine enough, but the old residents have flown and almost all the houses are now holiday lets, spilling children with bright plastic tractors and giant teddy bears out onto the cobbled lane.

Anyway, we enjoyed ourselves and came close again after a shaky three months. My fault. The result of the stupidest fling with an American curator, based in San Francisco.

Don't, on any account, breathe a word to Richard. I didn't tell him, and it's over, will never happen again. Too painful. And pathetic.

Really nice of Georgie to call by once a day to feed the cats while we were away. She's got two of her own, so has the cat touch.

With love

Lynn X

Mother

Couldn't I call you Mum again? That's how I think of you. Better-looking word too: Mum rather than Mother. I've been feeling my age.

My generation are so much ... so much HEAVIER than the next. Ten years makes such a difference in the arts. Their lot are funny, irreverent.

Gander's the prime example. Confined to a wheelchair by brittle bone disease. Does he care? Apparently not! Charges around like no tomorrow.

He and his friend Bedwyr Williams are showing in a gallery in Covent Garden, a video performance they call *Both Before and After, I Had to Write Your Obituary*, in which they've each invented a complete obituary for the other, as if published on Saturday 22 January 2050, within days of their separate conceptual deaths!

It's hysterical!

Well, it is if you're into art world innuendo.

Williams imagined the perennially sociable and anti-establishment Gander as a crack clay pigeon shot, spending his last years in resentful isolation and leaving 'a significant proportion of his estate to be held in care for his three Burmese cats Yvette, Carnedogg and Reuben.'

Maybe not quite as funny in the telling as viewing the video.

Love

Lynn

—

Lynn.
Stick to Mother, please, if you don't mind.
Thank you.
M x

[On a postcard with red letters on yellow ground, the word Library mutating into Liberty, published by Sheffield Library. Mum must have been up there sometime. She never told me.]

28 APR 08

Mother
Cocooned in my studio I forget how precarious things are for some artists. For everyone.
Another of the YBAs has committed suicide. Angus Fairhurst. Really nice man. I knew him a bit. Almost as critical as me about the art world. Though I didn't realise how tortured he was by disappointment, in himself.
Fairhurst went out for a walk in remote woods near Bridge of Orchy in the Highlands of Scotland, where he and his father used to hike when he was a boy, and hanged himself by a silk rope he had made for the occasion. His friend Gallaccio made the speech at his Tate wake, suggesting that his kindness, imagination and sense of humour be seen as inseparable from self-doubt. She told of her own period of darkness, in 1989, after her artist-brother hung himself, when Fairhurst never wavered in supportive friendship, a reliable presence even when there was nothing practical to be done to stem her sorrow.
Nothing more I can say.
A bit sad, isn't it, even though you don't know Angus from Adam?

155

You won't have lost your bar-lady compassion yet.
Love
Lynn x

12 MAY 08

Mother
I heard the other day, from Georgie, that Landy has a new project. Apparently, he's set himself the task of drawing sixty life-size portrait heads of invited friends over a fixed six-month period. One is of Georgie.
He works eight hours a day, five days a week. 'Like a proper job,' he says.
He needs four half-day sittings for each drawing, on consecutive days or with gaps, whatever suits. 'I feel like a hairdresser,' he said to Georgie. 'Taking appointments! "Sorry, can't cut your hair next week, love, I'm fully booked. What about the Tuesday after?"'
Landy's got it, no question.
Thanks for your letter. No more stuff about the Princess Di inquest, please. Leaves me cold.
Lynn XX

8 JULY 08

Mother
I love it when I unexpectedly come across a remark which echoes my own thinking.
Yesterday, in the drawings study room at the British Museum, I read an interview given last year by the American art historian Lucy Lippard: 'I like to work with artists who are trying to make a point about things in the world that I care about.'
Exactly.

I should be able to say such stuff for myself, without nailing to the page someone else to speak for me.
Is this me believing that well known others say things better than I do?
Or maybe I'm hijacking their reputation?
Regrettable, whichever way.
Love
from
Lynn x

3 SEPT 08

Mother
I'm trying to picture your flat.
What floor did you say it was on?
Must be a balcony. Do you sit out there in the evenings?
I don't really even know how hot it is on the Costa Brava in September.
Love
Lynn

[Written on one of the several large invitation cards which I had kept to Gilbert & George's show *The Naked Shit Pictures* at the South London Gallery in 1995, a colour photograph of the pair standing together looking up to the sky, in full frontal nudity apart from watches on their wrists and George wearing spectacles and holding a smoking cigarette in his left hand.]

26 OCT 08

Dear Mother
Something strange happened to me a fortnight ago. To do with my work. I need to write to someone about it,

and you're the person. Hope you don't mind.

I choose you because you're my mother and it's a secret, and I know you won't tell anybody. Because you wouldn't tell anyone anyway, even if I asked you to. And I'm not. I'm asking you NOT to.

For the first time in my life I saw an artwork which, in every detail, I would like to have made myself. Almost believed as I watched that I actually had made it. A film with the title *Ah, Liberty!*

By a man, seven years younger than me, called Ben Rivers. It's not just the film itself but the things he says about his work. That too could be me, almost word for word:

Throughout the drive through Britain the road is bare. Every now and then we come across a solitary older man, because I was into older men at that time and thought that's where I'm going too someday. They were going through their daily routines like the last remnants of humans, leaving some traces and clues for the future. Rivers wrote this about his short film *I Know Where I'm Going*.

I wish I'd made it, and written those words.

I'd like to meet him. Which is unusual for me. My rule of thumb is not to meet a writer or artist whose work I like, and risk terminal disappointment.

I saw *Ah, Liberty!* in Dublin earlier this month, at the Douglas Hyde Gallery in Trinity College. The curator of the exhibition wrote a booklet, several copies of which I bought, one here for you. Not that verbal description can touch the visual. You'll get the gist, all the same.

With love

Lynn

Ah, Liberty!
by Ben Rivers
John Hutchinson

Made by Ben Rivers earlier this year, *Ah, Liberty!* is a black and white 16mm film that ponders the idea of freedom. At a distance, but attentively, it gazes at some aspects of the liberated lives of a family in the remote Scottish countryside, paying particular heed to the children, whose habits seem to be especially carefree and unrestrained. But there is a shadow side to this idyll: wrecked cars are driven fast and carelessly through the fields and icy streams; junk lies abandoned in the otherwise unspoilt and beautiful landscape; a huge bonfire, comprised of rubbish and detritus, seems to burn incessantly. There is disorder at the heart of this place, and perhaps for that reason the film does not follow a linear narrative; it has no obvious beginning, middle, or end.

As is the case in many of Rivers' other works, *Ah, Liberty!* is a vision of a strange world hidden within our own, a world that is private, somewhat gloomy, and yet determinedly expansive and hopeful. These qualities are reflected in the way the piece is made, for although it is self-consciously grainy and wilfully imperfect, the film was shot on a wind-up Bolex in an anamorphic format that gives it a panoramic breadth. It is an odd and contradictory work, a cinematic essay that combines both unease and joy.

On first viewing, *Ah, Liberty!* may appear to be substantially true to life, but its 'realism' is actually more like a dream. It flows and holds together because of a consistency of tone, a predominant subjectivity, not because of its naturalism or documentary truthfulness. The structure is also more intuitive than natural; frames of white light

159

counterpoint the density of feeling, as well as providing a propulsive rhythm to the film. The soundtrack is illogical too, combining unsynchronised voiceovers with unexpected moments of silence, hints of equipment noise, and oddly inappropriate fragments of music borrowed from old movies.

A dark atmosphere pervades the film; the landscape, dogs, horses, wrecked cars, and fires all contribute to it. Some repeated motifs, such as the stormy, broody skies, and especially the children – wearing masks, dancing, breaking things – accentuate it. At the end, as in the beginning, there is a big blaze with sparks drifting into the night sky, and then, finally, a shot of the fire in the distance. The deep and dramatic monochrome, which is reductive and powerful, adds much to the menacing ambience of the film; its scratchy, stained, and burned textures help to sustain a mood of collapse and foreboding.

The script, brief and succinct, is cheerless. We are told that this is 'a young world, a world early in the morning of time, a hard, unfriendly world'; it is followed, later in the film, by an injunction to 'get off the world, get off the world, get off the world'. With its focus on children living in a grimly beautiful environment, *Ah, Liberty!* evokes William Golding's *Lord of the Flies,* and there are hints, as in the novel, that anarchy may be about to overcome order, and that innate savagery is not too far away. Fundamentally, though, the film's conception of freedom is benign; the children's primitivism is theatrical, their masks the expression of someone's imagination, not an expression of their innate brutality. As much to the point as their wildness is the moment of freedom and excitement when two children hurtle down a slope in a homemade buggy; as they take a bend too rapidly, part of it splits and turns over, spilling one of its occupants onto the ground. The camera watches dispassionately as the small boy bursts into tears and is comforted by his brother.

21 NOV 08

M

Me again.

Another thing about Rivers: he really is man-me!

Honestly! Every film I've by now seen of his could have been made by me. Same for him with my work, I bet you.

We do the same things. Read loads of novels. Go all the time to the theatre, contemporary music, all kinds of film, seldom opera or ballet. I've never met him. How could I have? I am him! And I've yet to meet myself. Much as I'd like to. Might make things easier!

Anyway, just to say I'm thinking of you. And the treatment.

Sounds like it's going OK?

Hope so.

Love from Lynn xxx

—

Dear Lynn

You're quite funny, sometimes.

I've been in hospital again 'for observation'.

Telling me! Not a moment's peace!

Skipped home in relief, catheter and all!

I'm planning to cut out spirits. Stick to red wine, as it's good for you, they say. Good for me. Essential!

My neighbour, Grania, has a key and stocked up my fridge, which was thoughtful of her. Like a good older sister. Except

she's younger than me.
And owns more swimming costumes.
Mind you, looks a dog's breakfast in them all!
Love
Mother

P.S. Perhaps you should meet this Ben chap. Keep Richard on
his toes.

29 NOV 08

M
Another of my lists for you.
Of artists aged forty or more who are friends of mine
and don't have children, male as well as female. In no
particular order.
Georgie, Gillian, Gilbert (not George, who has two
children he never sees, fathered before he met Gilbert),
Claude, Marijke, Suzy, Rebecca, Marjaneh, Richard,
Pauline, Tessa, Robert, Akiko, Michael, Paul, Cristina,
Helen, Lisa, Nikki, Corinne, Alison, Kathy, Keggie,
Frances, Mayana, Mark, Emma, Jamie.
That'll do. The list is endless.
Point made?
Love
L x

—

Dear Lynn
I've no idea what the point is you think you're making.
Whatever it is that you're on about it'll be critical of mothers,
as usual.
Critical of me in particular.

162

Go ahead. Water off a duck's back.

You've given up asking, so I'll tell you.

I never talk about my own mother because she was a bitch. Don't know why Dad put up with her. Talked down to him all the time, she did. And to shop assistants. Petrol pump attendants. Waitresses.

Nasty piece of work.

Remember the family things Betty talked to you about when you had that fancy lunch? Years ago, now.

She won't have told you half of what happened, because she doesn't know.

Doesn't matter now.

Being younger Betty got a better deal than me. Mother used to play duets with her. Made dead sure Betty didn't end up like me.

Love

Mother

12 JULY 09

Mother

Have I mentioned to you before an artist called Gavin Turk?

I'm pretty sure I did.

Anyway, he's proved my point, shown how it's possible to thrive without kowtowing to the art mafia.

He's made masses of work, seen internationally in dozens of exhibitions, group and solo, choreographed by the YBA power-broker White Cube. Work as small as a painted bronze apple core lying on the gallery floor, to as big as *Pimp*, an oversized black-gloss skip, glowering over the exhibition space.

My point? Turk has left White Cube, done a runner.

He's his own agent now. No fifty per cent commission. No changing colours to satisfy a millionaire's decorator.

No rabbit-run of corrosive art fairs.
Makes and sells what he wants, when he wants, to whomever he chooses, at prices he judges to be fair.
I hope SO MUCH he pulls it off.
Love
Lynn

—

Lynn
I don't get why dealers are such a big thing in art. What's so special about Turk selling his own stuff?
Seems to me the obvious thing to do.
All things being equal.
Mother x

[On a postcard titled *The Beautiful Island of Paxos. Refuse dump overlooking The Ionian Sea*, privately printed from a clandestine photograph and distributed free in tourist souvenir shops around the Med, the back stamped *Eco Fuck* and *This Postcard is Environmentally Unfriendly.*]

26 JULY 09

Dear Mother
I gave myself a birthday treat last night. On the day itself.
Bought a single ticket to see McKellen play Estragon.
He was incredible. Acted Stewart and Callow into the shadows.
Ronald Pickup held his own as the wordless Lucky.
It's that McKellen didn't 'act'. Well, he did act, of course, but doesn't show it. No Callow vowels, no Stewarty stares!
It's a privilege to be living in the same city at the same

time as Ian McKellen.
Love
Lynn

P.S. He's older than you!

—

L
Forgive me, I forgot!
Memory fried.
May have let the booze get a bit out of hand again.
Perhaps I should try yoga too!!
Love
M XX

[Mum sent this message on one of those maddening Trinity greeting cards, this one with a fat cartoon cat farting and the caption *Sorry, I'm an arsehole.*]

15 AUG 09

Mother
This is my happiest time of year, with the art world closed and silent across the globe. Nothing I need feel guilty about for not seeing.
Working the way I do, with little idea where research will lead, how my questions might begin to be answered, it's difficult to tell when the end is reached. Often continue planning and filming and writing for months longer than strictly necessary.
That's how it is, with me. I'm not complaining, the rewards have been fantastic. Beyond, way beyond

anything I expected.

With public access, the scale of the work grows. I hope not too much. Not bloated, swollen out of shape. It's ridiculous, I know, but with a full-time assistant now I feel under obligation to come up with ideas enough to keep her busy.

Why don't I tell her to work on her own stuff if I've nothing to be done?

I'll pay her anyway.

The new girl, Dharam, is my best assistant yet. A Sikh, dark-skinned, with the thickest of thick long black hair, she was born and brought up in Pollokshields and speaks with a broad Glaswegian accent. Bright as silver. I'm looking forward to seeing her tomorrow.

No exhibitions for the time being. My choice. To retrench.

My answer to all enquiries has been 'No'. The louder my no's, the more extravagant the offers and the firmer my determination to free myself from art world obligations.

It's been good talking to you in this letter, Mum.

Thanks. Thank you.

With love

Lynn

22 SEPT 09

Mother

The summer's flown.

With the new season about to get under way I spent an evening with Bridget, at her home in Bethnal Green. Small terraced house beyond the railway bridge, almost completely bare of art. Of everything except practical necessities.

Although she's been my dealer for thirteen years now

and I've visited her here dozens of times, the purity of the space always takes me by surprise. It's so unlike Bridget, you'd have thought, to look at and listen to her. Placed not the slightest objection to my wish to withdraw from the conventional marketplace.

It'll cost her. Same as it will me.

Bridget wanted to bring me up to date with the latest Beck Road news. She and her husband have been there for years. Since making the whole of the Southwark house into a gallery.

Her fellow-dealer Maureen Paley, one of the originals, still lives in the street, though many artist friends have moved on.

Helen Chadwick died too young. Bridget keeps in her office at the gallery one of Chadwick's last works, a letterpress print linking the words abhor and adore.

Alison Turnbull, Bridget told me, now lives in Kentish Town with her long-term partner, the Head of Byam Shaw School of Art.

And Genesis P-Orridge has recently concluded the Pandrogeny Project, started with his wife Lady Jaye, née Jacqueline Breyer. At vast expense – according to Bridget – they had surgery on their bodies and faces to make themselves look identical. Nose jobs, same shaped implanted breasts, all sorts. Both answering to the single name Breyer P-Orridge.

Genesis went on with surgery on himself even after Lady Jaye's death two years ago.

In Bridget's telling this somehow doesn't sound like the insider art-gossip it obviously is. Of utter unconcern to the world at large!

We drank pomegranate juice.

I wasn't late back home in Dalston.

With love, Lynn x

P.S. Afraid it may still feel to you that I'm dolling out contemporary art and film lectures in my letters. I do hope not. It's me self-talking, mostly. Which explains but doesn't excuse. It's just that I like describing these art things to you, fixes them in my mind. And then I can throw them out. Selfish, I know. I do everything for myself. Doesn't everyone?

12 OCT 10

Mother

I know you're not political. I'm not either, not in the party membership, campaigning sense. All the same, I'm incensed by the dominance in British politics of over-privileged, over-confident, over-paid, over-housed private schoolboys.

Aren't you too?

You would be if you were still in Birmingham. Guaranteed.

It's got way out of hand. Cameron and Clegg, the complete focus-group careerists. Royal Mail privatised. Free school milk scrapped. Twenty-five per cent reduction in public spending.

More and more unfair. And more to come, for certain,

When Cameron's father died last month, it turns out that all the family's assets were stashed, free of tax, in an off-shore company in the Bahamas! That's what the wealthy do, no question. Plain good sense, they say, to earn the absolute maximum amount of money on which to pay the minimum tax conceivable.

Convinced they deserve to be dozens of times richer than the rest of us!

Loathsome.

Totally unjust.

That's selfishness gone ballistic.

Shit! Done it again! Gone over the top.

Sorry, Mum.

To clear the air, here's a new Gilbert and George story for you!

Drink has played a significant part in their lives, especially for George. I like best the films they made in the early 1970s, in one of which a fixed camera filmed them standing at the bar in their local pub in Brick Lane, facing each other, chatting together and drinking. Until they were both so drunk that their words slurred to incomprehension and they had to hold onto the brass bar-rail to remain upright!

Anyway, when Richard was having dinner with them up the road the other night, he noticed that Gilbert poured himself a glass of water while George continued drinking red wine, as usual.

'Ahah! A difference!' Richard pointed out.

To which George instantly replied: 'Not at all. I'm perfectly happy for Gilbert to drink as little as he likes!'

Richard says that Gilbert burst into delighted laughter.

Seriously, I've learnt a good deal from G & G's early films. Their recent work has become too slick for me, but early on there's an unconventional lovingness. In the material quality of the film as well as their personal relationship.

I don't know how to express it properly. A warmth? Youth too. They were freer. Free to discover things. Weren't famous then.

Praise poisons more often than not.

Love

Lynn

P.S. It's seeing themselves as a superior breed which I

despise. Cameron and Clegg, I mean, not G & G. Like me and you, Mum, we're all the same, also the poor and the ill, the liars and cheats, terrorists and suicide bombers, murderers and rapists, druggies and drinkers. They're us, not them. Not 'animals', however dreadful the things they do. We're all just being human.

—

Dear Lynn
That's why I took to George that time I met him, at your wedding. Fellow drinker!
You can see why drink is the ex-pat bug. There's little else to do of an evening. Except go to bed. Which I'll never get used to doing alone.
I do sometimes wonder if I long-term did the right thing moving out here. Might've made more sense to get a small place in somewhere like Ramsgate. Rundown Brit seaside. I'd be more at home.
Have more money too. Could never afford to come back now.
It's not good, the way I live in L'Escala. I'm glad you've never seen it.
Doesn't matter.
I'll survive.
Love
Mother

P.S. Hoped you might have ridden your tired old hobby horse into retirement! Ten-a-penny twerps like Cameron and Clegg disappear without trace. Don't waste time on them, they'll be gone and forgotten in no time.

Mother

Yeah, apart from being gay, George is definitely your type. Likes to say what he thinks. His telephone answer message on the landline – they won't have a mobile – tells callers to leave their name and number, then ends 'Goodbye and good riddance!'

Didn't you leave for several months the recorded message 'I'm out. If urgent, try The Blind Traveller in Gilston Road'? That was before you worked there!

I've been enjoying the company of my proxy-niece, Fran, Annie's daughter. She's fifteen and telephoned me at eleven one night more than a week ago to say that if she remained a second longer in the same house as her mother, she'd have to strangle her! She turned up half an hour later in a minicab, with sky-blue fibreglass suitcase and her hamster Dingwall in a cage.

Been here ever since. I'll push her off back home on Saturday.

She's away all day at school and at weekends hangs out with friends. I don't know where. Don't need to. Fran's bright and lovely, she'll be fine.

To my surprise, I like Dingwall. Like the sound of the tumbrel turning in his cage as he tries, hour after hour, to run up its circling sides.

I've recorded the sound, the maestro element of which is the scrape of Dingwall's claws on the wire. I'm sure I'll find a place to use it.

Love

Lynn

FAMILY PORTRAIT OF TROUBLE IN
PARADISE

M
Happy fishing!
L xxx

[I made this specially for Mum. The found postcard is
of an idyllic country scene in Sussex, at either side of
which I've scalpelled a diamond and a heart shaped gap
and inserted at the back cut playing cards of queen and
king. From the queen of hearts trails a fishhook attached
to green cotton, reaching across the Downs towards
the diamond king. Can't remember where my collaged
title came from. Mum refused ever to tell me the date
of her birth, although in time I worked out that it must
have been sometime in December. Her age I knew and
that 2010 was therefore her seventieth year. I hope she
may have recognised that this was my version of a special birthday card, while respecting her right to silence
about the actual day.]

16 JAN 11

Mother
Last weekend Richard and I went to stay on the Isle of
Sheppey, with Lindsay and her partner Keith. Lindsay
is one the few people in the whole wide world I like staying with ... Ah, yes, don't need to tell you this!
Unusual place. At the entrance to the naval dockyard,
which is still owned by the Admiralty and half-emp-
ty. You have to halt at this old gatehouse to be allowed
in. Their house is beautiful: big, eighteenth century,

completely unaltered. It was the dockyard doctor's house and Lindsay's made her study in his vaulted surgery, with all her books.

Keith has done most of the restoration himself. It's going well, he says, except for the appearance of leaks in unexpected places during thunderstorms, with no immediately obvious cause. It didn't rain when we were there, fortunately.

We walked for miles and miles down the shingle, staring out at the grey on grey estuary and the North Sea beyond, past caravan sites.

She's my best friend.

Love

Lynn

5 FEB 11

Mother

You remember I used to work for Susan Hiller? Twenty years ago now.

Probably the most important artist-figure in my whole life, this formidable American who has lived in London since the early 1970s. I know people who're terrified of Susan. To me she's wonderful, as artist and person.

Wanted to tell you that Tate Britain have given her a retrospective.

I didn't go to the opening on the 1st, not even for Susan. She didn't mind at all, told me she wished she hadn't had to herself.

Anyway, I went yesterday and there's a vast installation of the postcards that she collected. Early postcards, mostly pre-1912, hand-tinted in the lithographic plate, of rough seas in seaside towns around Britain. Hundreds of them in their own big room at the beginning of the exhibition, multi-framed together with Susan's anthropological charts and lists.

She calls the work *Dedicated to the Unknown Artists*. To all those women – they mostly were women, of a certain age – who tinted the black and white photographs for local publishers around the coasts. Years before colour photography, with incredible precision of detail.

I thought of you. Of the postcards you bought when the two of us were on holiday. At St-Leonards-on-Sea, Robin Hood's Bay, Polzeath, once. Another year it was Butlins in Minehead.

Writing and posting. Writing and posting.

Who to, I wonder?

A bit late to ask!

With love

Lynn xx

21 FEB 11

Mother

A revelation!

Hadn't realised how helpful a good name is. Champion names like Ed Ruscha, or Nam June Paik. They can't fail.

I reckon being plain Lynn Gallagher was part of what held me back, to begin with. Joke!

Ruscha knew the value of his name. I've an invitation postcard of his in my collection, made in 1973, when he titled the show *Ed-Werd Rew-Shay Young Artist*, to emphasise the correct pronunciation.

Think of those Camden pals, Frank Auerbach, Lucien Freud and Leon Kossoff, they're all good Jewish names. What about their contemporaries with ordinary Anglo-names, ignored and forgotten. Maybe they also 'painted like deities'.

We'll never know now.

Painted like deities! What kind of idiotic comment is that anyway? Artist-worship by some fawning critic.

The name of Freud probably helped him pull all those women. Couldn't, I admit, have made him into the handler of paint he's become.

That's it, for today.

Love

Lynn

—

Dear Lynn

It's nonsense what you say.

Names have nothing to do with anything, unless you're talking about family. Come from the right family and you do all right. Not just artists. Crooks and drug dealers too. Politicians. Boxing promoters.

Keep it in the family, that's the game.

Look at Dynasty, *on TV. We often used to watch. Remember? That's how it works, the world over.*

Unfortunately.

Mother x

13 MAY 11

Mother

The posh word for what you're on about is patronage. Which makes it sound respectable. And it isn't. It's shit. You're right.

Nepotism, another clever dick word. Meaning the same thing. Give or take.

Love, Lynn

[With reluctance, I imagine, because I have always liked the postcard, I sent this message to Mum on a South Atlantic Souvenirs card, captioned on the front *Are you having the relatives for Christmas this year?*, above coloured anatomical drawings of human limbs chopped into roasting joints.]

20 MAY 11

Mother
Turk update.
He's unveiled a gigantic – twelve metres high – bronze nail stuck in the pavement outside an office block in the shadow of St Paul's Cathedral, by the French mega-architect Jean Nouvel. Commissioned by the developers. He told the *Guardian*: 'I suppose it's a nostalgia thing because I don't think there's a nail in the entire building.'
Love
Lynn

[I remember wondering whether or not to tell Mum the background to the Gavin Turk postcard on which I wrote this, and in the end decided to let the image speak for itself. She may have recognised Turk's adaptation of the Sun's front page on the eve of the First Gulf War, a British squaddie's head superimposed on a Union Jack, with the headline *Support our boys and put this flag in your window*. The youthful head is Turk's, the postcard self-published for his failed MA show at the Royal College of Art in 1991.]

—

Dear Lynn
I don't often write, not because I'm not interested.
I am.
I like you telling me about your art things, and the people, although there's really nothing worthwhile I can say in response.
Keep writing. I'm listening.
With love
Mother x

[On one of Mum's plain PO postcards.]

16 JULY 11

Mother
Whenever I see you – which, I admit, is hardly ever – we usually look at art together, somewhere or other, and you always make imaginative comments. Not-knowing doesn't matter at all. If you pay straight attention to what you see, you see it. If you see what I mean.
You do. You see. I can see that you do.
So I'll go on boring you about the things I see and you can't, while you loll in the sun on the Costa Brava!
It's Gander the magician and Artangel the ringmasters today.
They've made the strangest installation, in abandoned offices owned by the developers Londonewcastle, off the City Road.
Locked Room Scenario is Gander's apposite title. Very little work visible. Doors locked. Down at floor level a couple of awkward, narrow windows. Did catch the occasional glimpse of art-seeming objects through frosted glass and half-drawn venetian blinds, as I wandered down labyrinthine corridors with damp brown carpeting.
Near the exit, in a lobby, I came across a carousel

overflowing with multiple postcards and took two each of the four images.

On leaving, in impressed bewilderment, and crossing into Windsor Terrace on the way to the bus stop a woman tugged at the sleeve of my jacket and pointed to a folded piece of paper on the pavement behind me.

'No, it's not mine,' I said.

A smile from the woman, who acted dumb as she mimed the paper falling from the back pocket of my jeans.

I picked up the twice-folded page. Which had been torn from a book, with 'Mostly English; not too English' printed across the top and the phrase 'Aston's yellow mackintosh' circled in black biro in the text. Down the page a paragraph began in capital letters 'MARIE AURORE SORRY', and over the page the characters Vivi and Abbé were mentioned.

On the Artangel website for *Locked Room Scenario* a circled entry on the letter page reads 'MARY AURORY SORRY Vivi is dead ...'. And I recall that the name 'Mary Aurory' was graffitied on the wall in the yard at Londonewcastle.

Abbé Faria is the purported sculptor of *Barragan's Device*, the title-caption of one of the specially made postcards I pocketed.

The svelte young couple snogging on the stairs by the entrance must have been, I belatedly realised, part of the show.

Odd!

I do think, in general, that art is best consumed alone. Particularly something as puzzling as this. Easier without being aware of the presence of someone you know, distracted by concern for what to say to them, and what they might say to you. Stuck in Gander's bewildering installation, I drifted around in a haze of bemused suspense, loving my lack of comprehension.

I had arrived soon after morning opening time and no-one else was there.

Maybe the Artangel people on the door staggered entry, to enhance each individual's experience?

Theatre for one. I'm so glad I was alone.

Love

Lynn

2 OCT 11

Mother

We've learnt that those snorts and snores I told you about of Richard's in bed are caused by sleep apnoea. Cured, one hundred per cent, by wearing a face mask attached to a mini, almost silent motor blowing air into his nose and mouth.

It's interesting. Sufferers from apnoea apparently lack the normal mechanism telling them, when asleep, to continue breathing. In the worst cases – of which Richard is one – the breath-restart is left so late, close, in effect, to dying, that the convulsion sometimes throws them out of bed onto the floor!

Half-wakened, I used to assume he was having an especially horrid nightmare, turn over and go back to sleep. Anyway, everything's OK now.

No casual kissing when a plastic mask is strapped to your bloke's face, with a tube leading to a machine on his bedside table!

Sex by appointment.

Which means seldom.

Fine by me. And Richard.

Your own lovey-dovey days are over, I assume?

Lynn XXX

—

Dear Lynn

There's no law to say sex has to end at seventy, you know!

Anyway, depends on what you care to call 'performative' sex, as they say.

Or rather, depends on my definition. Which is, for sure, different from yours. Wider and ... No, best not go into our different levels of experience!

I'd heard about sleep apnoea, from a couple of men back in The Blind Traveller. You must make sure Richard cleans the mask regularly or he'll get sores on his face.

Nice face.

Give him my love

Mother

18 MAR 12

M

Good news.

Susan Hiller telephoned the other day to say that the Tate have agreed to buy her big postcard piece, with assistance from the Art Fund.

I should know what the Art Fund is, but don't. Some exclusive club or other. With their own private viewings, artist talks, guided tours of museums, New York to Tokyo via Berlin!

Anyway, Susan is delighted.

L X

[Instead of postcard or email, I wrote this note in pen on a piece of paper and sent it in an envelope with two elaborately hand-tinted old postcards. Bought them not long before from a charity shop in Minehead, both published around 1910, one of the interior of Chocolaterie Bonnet in Bristol, the other of waves breaking over the rocks at Anchor Head in Weston Super Mare.]

28 MAR 12

Mother
Jury service begins on Monday. Two weeks out of my life. And I've so much to do in the studio.
Got myself out of it twice before. No escape this time.
At the Inner London Crown Court in Borough.
You've never had to do it? Single mother bonus? Insufficient compensation, I'd say!
Ah well.
Love
Lynn

P.S. I've become addicted to Strepsils even though seldom actually having a sore throat. Mostly manage to restrict myself to the eight-a-day maximum permitted.

17 APR 12

Mother
Jury Service done. It was one of the worst experiences of my life.
Straight-up.
Knew as I was doing it that swearing allegiance to the Queen was a mistake. A lie, for certain.
Well, I've been punished for it.
Two Black boys, brothers, not yet twenty, up for Grievous Bodily Harm for a row in their local pub. Fighting some other boys, rivals since school. The older boy with a broken bottle, protecting his brother.

181

Their barrister was appalling, wig deliberately askew, arrogant voice, ill-informed, flushed in the afternoon with lunchtime drink. I had to stop myself shouting him down from the jury bench!

The mother testified. A nurse, soft spoken woman, who had brought up her children alone in Peckham and promised they were basically good boys, both of them in secure jobs, and that neither had been involved before with the police.

When we retired to decide the verdict, the others elected an officious little git as chairman. I failed to persuade him that the motives in a private brawl are incomprehensible from the outside and, by common law, therefore unindictable.

The result obvious from start-to-finish: the brothers found guilty by majority verdicts of ten to two and sent down by the judge for eighteen and nine months respectively. I and my solitary ally, the sales rep of a toilet supply company, shed silent tears as we retrieved our coats.

Are all establishments stupid and self-satisfied?

Christ! Jesus! Fuck!

Lynn

—

Dear Lynn

I don't know why, but I've been day-dreaming a lot outside on these sunny days. Sort of smoky scenes in the dreams, the point of which I can't quite work out. Don't in the least mind.

They seem to repeat, in altered versions.

Do see clearly the bits about my dad and the treats he used to set up for me and Betty.

The same every year, a lot of the time. Which was good, because

you looked forward to it even more, already knowing it was
something you loved. No fear of being disappointed.

Until one day you grew out of it. Suddenly didn't want to
go. Which upset Dad because he still wanted to. He didn't
understand.

You forget what it's like being young. At the same time as never
feeling anything like as old as you are.

I'm sorry now that I wasn't nicer to him.

The Royal Tournament was one of those treats of his. Down in
London at Olympia, during the summer holidays. I remember
best the motorcyclists, soldiers I think, doing complicated passing
manoeuvres, then roaring one after each other up a ramp and
through a flaming hoop, soaring through the air before landing
down onto the sawdust arena and speeding off through the exit.
'What a stunt!' Dad used to say, and clap loudly. Like men do.

There was a police dog display too, bringing to ground a pretend
criminal.

It was all always the same, as I say. Which we liked. Until we
didn't.

That's how it is.

Love

Mother x

20 JULY 12

Mother

My birthday this week.

Uugghh!

Whilst I'm none too happy being me, I certainly don't
want to be anybody else that I can think of.

Except perhaps Laure Provost.

It'd be great if I could be younger and able to make films
like she does. Raucous and daring.

We've both got short hair, that's a start.

It's not going to happen. Obviously, I'm not suddenly going to be thirty-five. I'm also never not going to be me. What I probably need to do is be as much me as possible. 'God forbid!'

It's OK I can hear you, Mum!!

Love, Lynn

12 SEPT 12

Mother

I think I wrote to you last year sometime about sex?

On my mind again. Can never work out what I think about it. Which may be the problem, as the point probably is to enjoy the doing and not think about it at all!

People, even couples, differ so much. George sometimes goes out cruising the East End streets at night while Gilbert always stays at home.

Gender doesn't define anything. Neither Richard nor I are much interested in sex at all. Whereas Richard's friends Jimmy and Karen think of nothing else.

Must be social, psychological. I really don't understand how it works.

You've always been keen on sex, and you're female, so it's not all manic men.

Maybe you still 'do it'? In reduced form.

Expert advice please!

With love

Lynn xx

—

Dear Lynn
I'm miles more interested in sex than art, that's for sure!
For the company.

You're not a people-person, never have been.
Richard neither.
I've come round to him, in time. He's a decent creature, not social
though. Stuck in his own world. Apologies for saying he was gay.
As I say, sex is people.
Yeah, I still help out the odd old bloke, now and again. Give
them a quick wank.
Men're the weaker sex, definitely, not us women.
I've this theory that not being able to give birth to babies is a big
thing for men. Unconsciously. Makes them feel inadequate and
so they hit back, by blaming us women for all their problems.
Love
Mother

—

L
When I was over in the summer you had more things on the
wall than the time before.
I meant to ask. What are they?
M xx

[On one of her Post Office cards.]

29 OCT 12

Mother
Yes, I had a bit of a spending spree last year. Adding to
the group of work I already own. Mostly then in folders,
now framed.
They're all drawings, by people I know. Or know of.
My favourite is the Landy. It's a self-portrait, drawn in
pink and black pencil, very delicately. Long title: *Radical*
Orchidectomy for a solid mass in the upper pole of the left testis.

185

It's a close-up, drawn in the mirror. Cradling in his hand his cock and balls, a recently operated scar livid on his shaved crotch.

Did you notice that mummy-like figure, which I call a drawing but is maybe more like a sculpture? The artist made it in memory of her just-dead father, gathering shells on the beach near where he lived, piercing a hole in each and stitching them to a cardboard torso. Then drawing lines on the clam shells with blue Chanel nail polish.

Some of the drawings are in our bedroom.

We have to be careful to hang them out of direct sunlight. Even though they're all framed in UVF glass.

Richard and I've agreed that we don't have to pre-agree, free to buy whatever we each feel strongly about. And can afford.

We mostly love the same things. Like the Jamie Shovlin, a watercolour drawing on a tear-out notebook, of one of his invented Fontana Modern Masters covers.

Jamie has such a speedy, vivid mind. Spotting that Fontana were ten short of their intended publication of fifty-eight paperback titles in the FMM series he filled the gap for them, inventing titles, authors and cover designs.

Ours is the imagined biography by Dr Jonathan Miller of Charles Sherrington, who won the Nobel Prize for Physiology in 1932.

Real people, fantasy book! Perfect fit!

Both of us adore it. We wake up and go to sleep to it.

I'll show you when you're next here. There'll be more by then, I expect.

None of my own stuff. Keep my working drawings in the wooden drawers of an architect's cabinet in the studio.

Love, Lynn xx

—

Dear Lynn
I never met the right man, that's my trouble.
Unlike Betty. Her Tony had a steady job all his life, without
ever interfering with B's career as a cashier at Lloyds.
Dead now. Bit of a letdown.
If I hadn't married your father, and had you, I could've been an
air hostess. Shown off my long legs and handsome bum.
Those were the days!
Might've met a sugar daddy. On stopover in Miami!
No complaints, all in all.
With love
Mother

P.S. Don't like to stir the pot, but aren't you turning into a bit
of a collector? Be nothing new for you to say one thing and do
another!

19 FEB 13

Mother
Was I more political as a teenager than other girls?
I can't remember any specific left-wing activism. No membership, or clubs or anything. I've never been a joiner, we all know that.
You're critical but not focused. And I'm both.
Focused in what I do and where I want to go.
I'll do anything at this stage to prevent my work falling into the hands of some non-dom, missile-procuring middle man.
Or amoral internet mogul.
On what else, in addition to buying art, do they spend their millions?

I'll tell you. They develop tourist resorts on unspoilt coastlines in Indonesia. Cattle ranches in the Amazon. Fly around the place in private jets. Run pay-little factories in Bangladesh. Own football teams, build golf courses. Speculate in the currency market. Put up high-rise towers of luxury flats.

International marauders, no boundaries for the super-rich,

Depressing. Best to step aside and live differently.

Lynn x

—

Dear Lynn

I'll tell you what. Do yourself a favour and stop banging on about rich people.

Gets you nowhere. Waste of time.

Don't have anything to do with them if you don't want to, just leave them alone and get on with your own thing.

Easy target, anyway.

You sound bored with the subject yourself half the time. Go on about it letter after letter. As tedious to read as the Guardian*!*

Mother x

1 MAR 13

Mother

I've taken up biking again.

A couple of times a week on fine days Richard and I go for a longish ride together. Usually across to the Millfields Park gate onto the Lea River cycle path, then over to the east side of Hackney Marshes and down to the Old Ford junction with the canal.

Following the towpath back towards home through

Victoria Park we often stop off for coffee at the cafe beside the lake. Read our books if it's sunny.

Lycra tights and hi-viz jackets banned. We do wear helmets, though.

With many more bicycles on the road these days I feel less vulnerable than before. Tend to take out my bike to do most things in town too. Not in the dark.

Lynn x

18 MAR 13

Mother

Saw this morning an ad in one of the art papers for an exhibition put on by a French-owned gallery based in Shanghai, taking place at an Irish-owned gallery in London, showing artists from Vermont, Taiwan, Istanbul, Galway and Tokyo!

How many air miles to bring that off!

Me xx

[With Mum's PO postcards in mind, I wrote this on one of a group of unique pieces I bought years ago, for very little, made by the Sunderland mail artist Robin Crozier in the early 1970s. He drew, in pencil, a small circle in the centre of a standard, printed Post Office postcard, writing below in his childlike rounded hand 'This is the exact centre of the universe.']

23 MAY 13

Mother

You asked about Bridget, if she's remained my dealer and if we're still friends.

Although she's a steady presence in my life, I'm not sure

I'd call her a friend.

After working through the inevitable misunderstandings, we've come to respect and trust one another. And we're each good for the other, me becoming the most critically acclaimed of her artists and she accepting that I simply am an unconventional figure.

We're ... what? Long-term working partners, you could say.

She wrote to me, only the other day, something so nice:

'I want the viewer of your work to feel that they are making a discovery, rather than being told by me what to think or feel in a heavily laboured or didactic way. It has always been my philosophy that, with gentle guidance, visitors to Mansfield Art should be given the opportunity to learn for themselves and take away something that hopefully will stay with them. The curator as intelligent enabler, no more.'

Very few people in the art and museum world think like that. I'm fortunate to have had Bridget beside me from the very beginning.

When things don't work out it's best, I feel, to cut off and move on. Even so, I've stuck with Bridget. And I'm glad I have.

Love

Lynn x

14 JUNE 13

Mother

What's happened?! You asked me to recommend half a dozen novels to read!

Makes me nervous. Where's the trap?

Camouflaged!

Let's see.

In no particular order: David Vann's *Caribou Island*, Anna Burns' *Little Constructions*, Lee Rourke's *The Canal*, Kader Abdolah's *The House of the Mosque*, Sylvia Brownrigg's *Morality Tale*, and William Trevor's *Death in Summer*.

Which, if any, will please?

Love

Lynn

[Written on an artist's postcard which I have always enjoyed by Jonathan Monk, titled *My Height in Blue Ballpoint Pen*, with a nearly straight blue line printed on a white ground, captioned on the back: *Install this postcard on any wall with the line six feet above the floor.* The postcard was published by the Lisson Gallery in 2003 in an edition of 200. On most birthdays from the age of about five till I left home, Mum used to push my back against the kitchen door frame, balance a book on my head and mark in biro my height on the chipped gloss paint. I remember her shouting at me: 'Stand straight! For God's sake!']

—

Lynn

You've got a nerve.

I was over from L'Escala, staying with Charmian, who's moved to Solihull. She took me to see your exhibition at Ikon, across the canal from Symphony Hall.

That's the last straw. You can't be bothered to tell your own mother about films of yours and talks and events in Birmingham? Knowing I came down under my own steam to see those London shows of yours?

That's it.

Count me out from now on.
Mother

8 JULY 13

I should have told you, I'm so sorry.
Honestly, I didn't think you'd want your friends to see my films. And I'd no idea you'd be over yourself.
Lynn

[One of my self-made cards, put together from the found postcards I keep in a drawer in the studio, this one published in 1964, of the Beinecke Rare Book & Manuscript Library at Yale, holders of the James Joyce archive. With a thin brush I painted in red capital letters across the bookstacks this quote from *Ulysses*: 'A flying sunny smile rayed in his loose features.']

16 JULY 13

Dear Mother
Have you forgiven me?
I don't really deserve to be, but I hope you have.
Art things are going my way and I'd like you to feel part of it, in some form.
To coincide with the Ikon show, *Frieze Magazine* interviewed me. It came out better than I was afraid it might. I agreed only on the condition that the conversation would be published verbatim, bar mutually agreed edits. There was some bad-tempered discussion about the morality of the art world. This got a bit out of hand, with me slagging off Frieze Art Fair, and we agreed to cut this out.
With love, Lynn

P.S. I think that the three illustrations, printed three-quarter page as I insisted, look suitably puzzling. Too much so? Better than the eight smaller images the editor failed to persuade me to accept!

Renegade
Lynn Gallagher talks to Kirsty O'Callaghan

KO: On the eve of your major exhibition at Ikon, I'd be interested to know where you see yourself in the pantheon of contemporary British art.

LG: I don't.

KO: Could you elaborate?

LG: No.

KO: In that case, shall we talk about the Ikon exhibition? You're showing your new full-length feature film *The Sky Trembles And The Earth Is Afraid And The Two Eyes Are Not Brothers*. Full-length title! What's it about?

LG: Despite being set in Morocco, this is a very personal film, in which I worry, especially in the second half, about how I dare to make films at all, dare to presume to place more statements out into the already saturated world of much better ideas than mine. Two opposed aspects of my own character, the capacity for clinical observation and a tendency towards intense absorption, fight it out in this movie.

KO: It's ...

LG: Sorry, I meant to say that, as often in my work, I make use of a literary text for support, not usually in a form recognisable to anyone other than myself. In *The Sky Trembles* the hovering demon is Paul Bowles, in his troubling short story 'A Distant Episode'.

KO: Although the Ikon display includes drawings, both self-sufficient works and preparatory sketches for films,

193

still photos, models, props and even personal ephemera, the central emphasis is, in my view, on the moving image. Do you agree?

LG: I do, yes. I'm essentially a filmmaker. Limited in what I can do, like everyone else, because I'm confined to myself. Someone once said to me that Fellini said something along the lines if his inspiration was one day exhausted, he'd make a film about exhaustion! I mean, I'm not desperately keen on Fellini's movies but I admire and share his attitude to filmmaking.

KO: About another of your films showing, *It Has To Be This Way*. I'm slightly confused. Are there several versions? Not that it really matters. I loved the screening at Ikon.

LG: Yes and no. The numbering one to five generally refers to the books published at different film venues, the authorship attributed to friends though heavily drawn from my own writings.

KO: I've read three of these. They're all amazing in different ways. I was particularly moved by the Matt's Gallery edition of 2010, which claims to have been written by someone called M. Anthony Penwill, but sounded as I would imagine your own writer-voice to be. The troubled sister, Christine Parkes, could be you too. Especially as an endnote reads: 'The selection was made from photographs in the archive of Lynn Gallagher/Christine Parkes.' Might you elucidate?

LG: [laughs] You ask so nicely! In principle I'm against explanations. My stuff is whatever anybody else, everybody else, thinks it is. I assure you, though, Penwill exists. He lives in the town where I was brought up and went to school. The text was written according to the content of thirty photographs chosen by me, the order selected at random by others. Which means, if you believe in photographic truth, that everything depicted is contingent on events which must have happened in some form.

KO: Thank you! And *Two Years At Sea*?

LG: This is another example of my being pulled to remote locations, actually a place, in the Scottish Cairngorms where I've stayed many times. The film itself was made during five different visits, covering the four seasons. It's based around the life of my friend Jake, who lives on his own in the woods, largely self-sufficient, spending the evening hours reading and listening to his inexhaustible store of music. My favourite bit is the seven-minute shot of Jake floating across the lake on a self-made raft, buoyed on air drums. And the ending as he watches his bonfire on the beach burn out, slowly falling asleep and disappearing into the grain and blackness of the film. *Two Years At Sea* presents a person who is not exactly Jake but similar to him, someone who isn't seeing anyone, who is solitary but not lonely.

28 JULY 13

Mum
I wasn't sure about Renegade as title of the *Frieze* article. Now I really like it. Seems – to me – like me!
Does it read OK?
Lynn xx

[Another Queen E II and Duke of E collage of mine, a postcard of the couple in an open carriage on their way to Trooping of the Colour, with a serrated white rectangular patch obliterating the monarch's head, on which I have printed *Affix Stamp Here.*]

Mother
You're expert in this field. Why does male piss stink?
Mine doesn't.
Does it?
Maybe we can't smell our own urine? Like not being
able to see our own faults.
Ha! Ha!
Not very funny, I agree.
Lynn xx

[Written on the back of an unused original Bamforth
postcard of 1915, an anti-pacifist publication with the
lithographed image of a soldier with a pock-marked
potato as his head and the caption *I've summat to swank
about; I'm going to the 'trenches' – and that's more than some
of you are doing!*]

—

L
It all smells, some people's sweet, others' sour.
*You can drink a healthy specimen of human piss. Better for you
than Fernet Branca!*
M X

[On a Klaus Staeck anti-smoking postcard, of five cigarettes poking out of the top of a pack, each fitted with
a three-pronged barbed fish hook. No idea where Mum
picked this up, designed and published by an important
German postcard man.]

Mother
We haven't set eyes on each other for ages. Would you like to fly over to stay for a week or so?
I'm not going anywhere now till the second week of November. Then I'll be away almost till the end of the year, in Zanzibar for some filming, and back via Tel Aviv to see Lia van Leer. Old now and unwell, probably the last chance I'll get of spending time with her.
Lia is one of those tens of thousands of Israelis whose histories sound medieval, barely believable as contemporary, despite all we now know. When she was sixteen, in Bessarabia in 1940, her parents sent Lia to stay with her sister Bruria, a dentist, who had emigrated to Palestine in 1936. They never saw their parents again.
Lia chose not to become a mother herself.
Like Susan, only differently, she's been a special force-for-good in my work, twice showing me at the Jerusalem Film Festival. She still works part-time at the Cinematheque, which she and her husband founded in 1973.
I want to show her trial sections of *Nowhere Less Now*.
Yes, lots to do. As usual. Luckily.
Hope I can see you before I leave.
Love
Lynn

—

Dear Lynn
Of course you can see me! You just have to go to Cambridge for Betty's 70th, as she's asked!
Afternoon of October 25th, at the Garden House Hotel.

Overlooks the Cam, she says. Sounds extra-smart to me.
Close enough to her house.
Why are you being so difficult about it all? Betty'll never for-
give you if you don't go. Nor will I.
Mother x

8 OCT 13

Mother

I forgot, sorry.

No, that's not entirely true.

I didn't know how to tell Aunt Betty that I badly don't want to go. You know how I dread parties of any sort, family gatherings most of all. Now I've left it too late to explain!

O-o-o-h-h ... okay, I'll go!

At least I'll be seeing you.

Though I will NOT stay in Betty's or anybody else's house. Am right now booking myself a single room at the Garden House Hotel itself, whatever the cost.

Suppose I could arrange to see the people at Kettles Yard the next day?

Maybe I could persuade them to host a future screening of my films in a fun location. At the Botanical Gardens, for instance. Or the Real Tennis Court on Grange Road. In James Stirling's great lecture hall in the History Faculty!

Mmm, I'm coming round to the idea of this excursion!

With love

Lynn

—

Dear Lynn

Betty and I went to The Fitzwilliam when I was in Cambridge. My first time. Lovely small museum. They've got several Richard Long drawings, of driftwood on the Severn, and things. Beautiful, I thought.

So when I arrived back home and heard he had a show on at the CaixaForum in Barcelona, I went in by bus. Last week.

Why haven't you ever mentioned Long? Too straight for you lot?

If that's what you think, you're wrong. He's an original, I reckon. His line in the grass, that's major. Surely?

I'm sure it is, whatever you say.

And the circles of slate?

Well, I don't like them as much, that's true. He's best with the stuff he does outside.

See you

Love

Mother

P.S. Too annoyed to tell you at the time, but Charmian really liked your show at the Ikon Gallery. And she's into art. One of the reasons we're friends.

5 MAY 14

Mother

A touch of serendipity.

I love it when things like this happen. Good word too!

For several months now I've been reading *Ulysses*. Last night in bed, taking a break from Joyce and turning to Mary Costello's *The River Capture*, I came across back-reference to Bloom's partiality to the smell of cooked kidneys, which chimed directly with a Joyce passage I'd copied months ago into my quotes notebook.

Set in the Irish countryside of today, Costello describes her lead character Luke's hero worship of Joyce and places this remark in the mouth of one of his clever pupils: 'Sir, there's a tang of faintly scented urine off my sandwich.'

My Joyce note reads: 'Mr Leopold Bloom ate with relish the inner organs of beasts and fowls. He liked thick giblet soup, nutty gizzards, a stuffed roast heart, liver slices fried with crustcrumbs, fried hencod's roes. Most of all he liked grilled mutton kidneys which gave to his palate a fine tang of faintly scented urine.'

I don't know, maybe this is a famous passage? What I do know is that I'd never personally come across it before, not until turning that page in February. Laughed out loud. Loudly!

And now the Costello coincidence.

Susan would see the spirit world at work.

There's no-one like Joyce.

That's absolutely the only thing I'm grateful to my father for. His being half-Irish.

Are you sure you're not partly Irish, somehow? Then I could take half from each parent, drop the British bit, and make myself fully Irish!

With love

Lynn

16 JUNE 14

Mother
Bad news, I'm afraid
Very.
Richard has to have a gastrectomy. He's been in pain for ages but didn't tell me. It's nerves, anxiety. That's how he is. A forest of polyps has grown on part of his intestines,

which they'll have to cut out. He should be OK.

Nothing's certain.

I'm twice as worried as he is. Four times. He's such an undramatic man.

All right for him, if anything goes wrong, he'll be dead. What about me? He might at least try to survive.

We'll see, we'll see, as I'm always saying.

I think maybe I have an ulcer. How do you tell?

Can't stop thinking of Richard's mother, thirty years buried at the Kirk in Leith.

Love

Lynn

—

Lynn
Don't be such a pessimist. I'm sure he'll be OK.
With love
Mother

P.S. Is Richard Scottish? He doesn't sound it.

[Written on one of her now slightly faded, standard-blank Post Office cards, from several packs Mum must have taken over to Spain when we cleared her flat in Sparkhill.]

30 JUNE 14

Mother

You never tell me what you think of the novels I recommend, merely from time-to-time ask for more suggestions.

Doesn't matter. The reading of books is the most private

act I can imagine. Especially a new book. Reading a book untouched by anybody else, however many thousands of other copies may exist, it's intimate, undisturbed.

I feel safe when I'm reading.

You could try Graham Swift's new novel *Mothering Sunday*. And I really liked Sara Baume's *A Line Made by Walking*, which I bought because of the title, taken from the Richard Long work. You'll like that!

I took down a Baume quote, to keep me up to scratch!

'Here I am. Perceiving everything that is wonderful to be proportionately difficult, everything that is possible an elaborate battle to achieve. My happy life was never enough for me. I always considered my life to be more precious than that of other people and almost every routine pursuit – equitable employment, domestic chores, friendship – unworthy of it. Now I see how this rebellion against ordinary happiness is the greatest vanity of them all.'

If you can get hold of it, try Alana Jelinek's *The Fork's Tale*. Fun, written from the point of view of a table-fork!

You probably don't read Nigerian writers. A pity, as I think you'd like a lot *Half of a Yellow Sun* by Chimamanda Ngozi Adiche.

I'm over halfway through *Ulysses*. Still loving it.

Less keen than to begin with on the Costello novel. The last hundred pages are in the form of self-questions by the irritating Luke. Joyce pulled this device off but she doesn't, in my view.

Love

Lynn

—

Dear Lynn
Don't get me wrong, I'm glad to have those recommended books
to read. They're company. Some of them.
Make me think, at least.
I'll try the Baume. Won't bother with Costello. Luke's not my
kind of name. Smart-arse, I bet.
Mother xx

[Written on a Spanish tourist postcard of Gaudi's
Sagrada Familia, a detail of the tops of those incredible
spires, in evening light.]

2 AUG 14

Mother

I'm on my fourth visit this summer to Frankfurt, working with Portikus on an installation. Not in their gallery,
great building though it is, but off-site. Location is inte-
gral to the work, and we finally found the perfect place.
A two-storey tin cabin in Kaiserlei, east of the city centre, beside a functioning wharf right on the river. Till
recently a training centre for German Sea Scouts.
Final touches before opening next week.
It's a great place, set out inside as if on and below deck
of an old navy ship, complete with bridge and steering
wheel, cabins and galley, decorated with ropes and flags
and other nautical memorabilia, most of which I've kept
in place unchanged for my show.
Working here has been a pleasure.
When it rains the sound on the tin roof is magnified inside. A touch intimidating. Seems to make people pay
closer attention to my installation!
Nowhere less now may be the best thing I've ever
done. Strange that elements of Susan's extra-sensual

perception, which I wasn't aware of much admiring when I was her studio assistant, have emerged in the film element of this piece.

Love

Lynn

P.S. Here's the booklet Portikus are publishing. Don't choke on the 'Great Great Uncle George' stuff. Lindsay loaned me the information on him, and the memorabilia. She was born in Zanzibar, I think. No, that's not right. Lived there once, definitely. Not definitely. Nothing's definite, is it? Not with me, anyway!

P.P.S. The illustrations are not those I would have chosen myself, although I can see how these images do fit with the Portikus aesthetic.

Nowhere less now

by Lynn Gallagher, Piers Kingston,
Elaine de Rougemont, Ole Hagen

The text of this small book relates to Lynn Gallagher's Portikus installation by the River Main in Kaserlei. It is not a script for the film content, nor is it an exegesis of the work. Rather it *is* the work, an extension of it into another medium. Gallagher's creativity declines the dichotomy of fact and fiction, because nothing seems to her entirely factual or entirely fictional. Fictional implies untrue and she is looking for the truth in things which supersede mere factuality.

Starting with the question 'Where does the past exist?', the project tells a many layered story through the agency of composed film and photographs, found historical ephemera, architectural constructs, existing material

204

belonging to the German Sea Scouts, and a lengthy essay by Dr Ole Hagen, Senior Lecturer at Brighton School of Art. The installation responds exponentially to three separate elements of inspiration: Gallagher's research; her own philosophical and biological concerns; and the qualities and contents of the Frankfurt site. The small cabin displays objects, some left *in situ* by previous occupants of the hut, others made by Gallagher to embroider her tale. The largest space at the Sea Scout headquarters is dominated by Gallagher's reconstructed hull of a boat, upturned as if to tip out its dark secrets. This is modelled on the black-hulled ship HMS Kingfisher, on which the artist's Great Great Uncle George was an able seaman, and which was moored for ten years in the bay of Zanzibar as a depot for the anti-slave mission. Inside this space, Gallagher's two-channel projection opens by introducing a narrator, Ina, a Spanish dancer raised in Germany. The early scenes show Ina dancing on the shores of the German island of Heligoland in the North Sea, after which a succession of realisations leads to Leni Riefenstahl's Nazi film *Triumph of the Will*.

The filmic installation, which lasts for twenty minutes, weaves back and forwards in time, returning to connections with nineteenth-century Zanzibar and its exhibited memorabilia, including the photograph of a youthful George Edwards in a formal group with fifty of his fellow sailors on HMS Kingfisher. Gallagher appears to suggest that close inspection of reality leads inevitably to the discovery of the end of a thread that, when tugged upon, will unravel the world's historical chains of causation and consequence. Her film enmeshes us in a net of associations and connections, traces of the past that has formed the present and will shape the future. Searching for connections, we find them, she shows.

At one stage, on a trip to Zanzibar, Gallagher dressed up as Georgina, her Great Great Uncle's wife, and is filmed wandering down side streets little changed since the 1880s. Others appear in the film costumed and made-up as sailors, women as men, as a liberated slave and as an Arab princess in the company of a young English sailor drifting in the currents of Empire. The film is neither beautiful nor poignant. It touches no sentimental chords but, masterfully woven together and deeply original, there is something piercingly compelling about it.

The text and illustrations of Ole Hagen's book elucidate and confuse, written in the first person, describing the author's observations on the creation of *Nowhere less now*. Some passages are clearly addressed to, or are about, Gallagher, but there are also lengthy sections when the 'I' seems to be the artist herself – though this may be an act of deliberate ventriloquism by Hagen, aware of Gallagher's interest in this subject. Much of the book dwells on the belief that a dead human-being can remain alive in some communicable way. Hagen wrote: 'Lynn started to talk about this strange idea that maybe our dead relatives could be alive somewhere in the future. She thought that walking into the future might be just like walking into another room, and if our ancestors could do that, they might have something to tell us.' Later in the book he seems to transcribe Gallagher's account of seeking to make combined visual and verbal contact, not only with her Great Great Uncle George, but also with others named George Edwards:

'This time I submerged the photograph in a tray of ink, while writing a message again on the surface of the water. I took another photograph as it emerged floating on the black inky surface. I scanned this and opened it on my desktop. I made a flipped version of it in Photoshop and wrote the message again on the back with a virtual-pen tool, thanking George for contacting, telling him to do what he had to do, and asking in turn what I could do for him.'

As with the majority of Gallagher's work, there is a strong feminist ingredient in the narrative, one element being the presence of Moina Mathers – sister of the French philosopher and mystic Henri Bergson – who was married to a co-founder of the esoteric organisation Golden Dawn, one of the first of such groups to admit female members. An addict of connectedness, Gallagher points out that Mathers studied at the Slade School of Art.

The images in Gallagher's films are projected on to two screens, one flat and round, the other spherical, symbolic, of the fact that one of Great Great Uncle George's eyes was green the other blue, a medical condition explored by the artist in her earlier work, *Different Coloured Eyes*. The double screens are suggestive of human eggs and also of portholes, the montages symptomatic of Gallagher's restless search for truths that remain elusive as they slip through the lens. One event leads to another in a world where coincidence takes on the character of necessity. The unfurling narratives project forward as well as backwards: from a young English sailor drifting across the oceans, to the inscription on a centuries-old Baobab tree in Zanzibar, to a future when dates have become irrelevant and photography is redundant.

Gallagher has commented on this work: 'Reflecting a decentred idea of selfhood that has many moods is central to my work: abstract, virtual, documentary, constructed and deconstructed. It is a fiction we require: to believe ourselves and the world to be consistent.'

Lynn Gallagher is one of the most exciting filmmakers to have emerged in Britain over the last ten years. With *Nowhere less now* we are in the presence of an important work by an artist of stature.

28 AUG 14

Mother

I've been thinking a lot about the contrast between working with Portikus and the power nuts at Hauser & Wirth. It's not healthy, I know, the way the same thoughts race round and round my head. Getting louder and louder, making me angrier and angrier.

What can I do?

It's SO wrong how Hauser & Wirth work, and yet the world glorifies them.

Now they've opened an arts centre in Somerset, where these Swiss billionaires farm a thousand acres and sell Phyllida Barlow installations for a hundred times more than she dreamt of asking before, during a forty-year career.

I've nothing against Barlow. Far from it. She's been an influential teacher at the Slade for decades, set Whiteread on the right road. In no way do I begrudge her the attention for installations which are bold and brave. It's the money!

All the 'community outreach' and subsidised café and free talks, all of this H & W tosh, it's a front, a deceit. Their primary focus is on selling art at gargantuan sums of money.

Got it out! I feel better now!

Let's move on.

Love

Lynn xx

L

It's such a bore, your anti-money gripe.

Same old thing. On and on. Art market or the city, nothing new.

Why can't you behave like every other sensible person and accept the going rate for your work? If that's more than you think is right, then give the extra to me.

What's Wirth worth?

You've got me going now!

Sounds a greed freak, grant you that.

Don't forget, you've always wanted a lot too. In a different way. What's so wrong with being successful? That's what I'd like you to tell me.

M x

14 SEPT 14

Mother

Looks as though the Frankfurt installation will be bought by a German collector with his own museum, open to the public. Unaltered, in its entirety, tin cabin and all. He complained at my restrictive conditions. No choice, if he wants the piece. Which he does.

The curator of his collection asked me to do talks and press interviews and video links. More-or-less insisted. Got her nowhere.

I can't express it better, anything I say now could only make it worse, I told her.

They came round.

It's my time, I'm in charge. Another time will come when nobody cares about Lynn Gallagher. Which is fine. I'll still be in charge.

209

I don't think I've ever told you this but one of the things I found so very difficult at home when I was young was there being only me, the centre of your attention. It frightened me. Everything noticed. Nothing my own. You being in total control of me.

Didn't show it, would only have made it worse.

If I had to be alone with you, I wanted not to exist.

It's OK, I never tried to ... to do it.

Any special stuff that I had you always found. And confiscated.

It was bad. Really bad.

I'm OK now.

I'll be OK from now on in. So long as I keep the art world at a distance, don't lose control. And keep my anger in proportion.

With love

me x

—

Dear Lynn

You DID show it!! Made it obvious you couldn't stand me! Why do you think I let go of you without a fight? It was a relief by then to get rid of you.

I know I made a fuss later, when everything went pear-shaped for me. Suddenly needed you and you wouldn't come home.

Looking back, I can see how things get fixed solid. Time passes. Months and years go by so much quicker than one realises. In no time it's set in stone. That's how it works and there's no turning things around.

Yes, it was bad, but we got by in the end.

We're strange creatures. Not just us, everyone. Things get so sad that it feels impossible to go on, and yet we survive, carry on in the end as if nothing had happened.

I don't really understand anything. Not a single thing!
Which is more-or-less what you wrote to me once. If I remember
right.
Love
Mother

28 SEPT 14

M
When I was a child you seemed to me to resent my pres-
ence in your life.
And I gave up.
Not easy.
Better than giving in.
L x

[On a postcard printed with a large thumb print in black
on white, or maybe the other way round, captioned *Black
or White?*, published in the 1980s by the Minority Rights
Group.]

26 NOV 14

Mother
Richard's fine. He's back home, the operation went per-
fectly. I was stupid to panic.
The wait for surgery was difficult but doesn't matter now
that he's going to be all right.
Love
Lynn

[This was written on an old seaside postcard that had
been in my store-drawer for ages, of two grey kittens in
a saucepan and the caption *Pot Luck from MEVAGISSEY,*

with a concertina of ten black-and-white views of the Cornish fishing village falling from a flap on the front.]

Mother
You can't beat Joyce for adjectives. I read this in bed this morning, on page 382 of the Bodley Head hardback edition of 1980:
'The figure seated on a large boulder at the foot of a round tower was that of a broadshouldered deepchested stronglimbed frankeyed redhaired freely freckled shaggybearded widemouthed largenosed longheaded deepvoiced barekneed brawnyheaded hairylegged ruddyfaced sinewyarmed hero.'
He's bonzo. Pity about the syphilis.
Lynn xxx

P.S. Mind you, William Blake was no slouch with words either. Never forget when I was a student, seeing in the Tate archives a drawing of his captioned in his own hand 'Vegetating in fibres of blood'. Two hundred years later we're into wonky sharks and think that's daring!
P.P.S. You asked not long ago what I thought it meant to be a success in art. My answer: being James Joyce or William Blake! Add Boulez in music and Beckett in theatre. Clear enough?

—

Dear Lynn
Did Betty tell you she's moved into sheltered accommodation? Small bedroom and sitting room, with en suite bathroom. All her own furniture.

212

Beautician calls once a month to do her nails. Lovely long fingers, Betty.

Someone turns up from Cambridge to fix her hair whenever she asks.

Meals in the dining room with the other residents. And a comfy communal room with regular activities, plus state-of-the-art TV and an upright piano. She plays, in the early afternoons when there's nobody around. Her usual razzmatazz.

She's younger than me.

You know that, of course.

Plenty of money.

Makes me wonder how long I'll be able to carry on looking after myself.

No choice. Could never afford a Home.

Can I come and live with you? In the basement?

No, that's a silly suggestion. It'd never work.

I'll be all right.

With love

Mother

18 MAR 15

Mother

I find it difficult to see you, or myself for that matter, or Betty, ageing.

Makes no sense that I spend my life staring through the lens of a movie camera, making the minutest visual adjustments, taking account of the tiniest changing detail in the light, and yet fail to register that I no longer look twenty-two!

I haven't seen you since Aunt Betty's 70th. Please come over soon. I'll send you the ticket money today. And extra.

Best to talk through Home things face to face.

Let me know if there's some theatre on that you want to see, and I'll book. Anything else you'd like to do? Georgie said some time ago that she'd be curious to meet you. We'll go and have tea with her and Gary, in the Georgian townhouse they've bought in Clerkenwell. Five floors and a garden!

You'll see!

One evening we can walk down to get fish and chips at Faulkners on Kingsland Road, afterwards to a movie at the Rio.

Richard and I go as often as we can. To both.

Best fish and chips in town, and the Rio is a co-operative, run by locals.

Much love, Lynn

11 MAY 15

Mother

I'm so very glad you came over. Thanks a million.

Glad too that we've sorted out future living.

Georgie told me how moved she was seeing us both together, after hearing so much about you from me over the years. She said that, when we left, she sat down in one of those red armchairs by the sitting-room fireplace and cried. I know what she was thinking. I'd like to tell you, but mustn't. Betrayal of confidence.

Oh yes, thank you tons for the candlesticks. How did you know I liked them so much? Won't you miss them? I remember you bargaining at that bring-and-buy market in Solihull, giggling with the man on the stall at the pair being made of old tiddlywinks!

What was the joke?

I must have been about ten. We did everything together then.

You didn't have to tell me about the stuff with your mother. I'm really grateful, though, that you did. Everything for Betty. Cut you out of her life. Explains a lot.

You've done so well, Mum. For yourself. And for your daughter. For me.

Richard sends his love. It matters to me that the two of you get on.

With my love too

Lynn xx

—

L

Please don't badger me about my shoes.

They may be scruffy but they're comfortable. I feel safe in them, as a matter of fact. Less likely to take a tumble.

When you get to my age that's important. Broken hip and I'm done for. Hospice and bedpans for the rest of the stretch.

The older you get the less you need. One thing you particularly don't need is change. Like new shoes. You look down at your feet and can't recognise yourself.

Thanks

M XX

—

Dear Lynn

I'm remembering my visit and you and the coffee testing. Made me smile. So typically you!

There in the kitchen you'd five samples of coffee. Unground. From Monmouth in Borough Market, I think you said?

'Time we tried something new,' you insisted. 'Blind tests.' Poor Richard, all he wanted was a quick black espresso and to slink back to his study!

215

And in the end the one you were totally certain was the best turned out to be the coffee you'd been drinking for the last three years.
So funny!
With love
Mother

8 JUNE 15

Mother

Absalom is dead and buried, beside the garden fence.

He was ancient. A shock, nevertheless.

I came home from the studio at about eight one evening last week and he was laid out on the kitchen floor, legs straight. Knocked flat by a heart attack, no pain, it seems, his mouth closed, no sign of a stifled scream.

Lindsay happened to be staying the next night, which was a comfort. She had meetings with some Charity or Trust or something, in Pimlico.

I'm tired.

Off to bed.

Love

Lynn

—

Dear Lynn
Good that you've got a friend like Lindsay. How's she doing in Sheppey? I once spent a week's holiday in Southend-on-Sea, on the opposite bank of the Thames.
With your dad, it was.
You might have been there too, a babe-in-arms.
Can't remember.
There's an awfully long pier at Southend, and a model steam

216

train with bench-type open seats facing to the side. Takes you to
the café at the end. And a lifeboat museum.
Say hi to Lindsay from me.
Friendship is what matters, not sex. A sister who is also a friend
is the best. Like Betty.
Not an option I gave you. Makes Lindsay extra-special.
Love
Mother

21 JULY 15

Mum
I can't believe it!
Have to tell you.
I had a meeting the other day at Bloomberg, in the City.
They're ... actually I'm not quite sure what they are.
Thought they were a bank, but apparently not ... Let's
say financial services. Covers sufficient iniquities!

Anyway, Bloomberg has been involved in contemporary art things for years and they approached Bridget to
see if I'd accept the commission for a quadruple screen
installation in the atrium of their New York head office.
The meeting went well, until, while we were having a
break for coffee and croissants, the Bloomberg pair, two
middle-aged men in ocean blue suits and whiter-than-
white shirts, began to reminisce about their fathers'
wartime experiences.

One of them told the other of his father describing the
cruelty inflicted on him by the Japanese when he as a
prisoner-of-war, aged twenty.

His colleague responded, very reasonably: 'Nothing
compared to the Americans H-bombing the citizens of
Hiroshima one night and Nagasaki three days later!'
The first man, the one wearing a pink tie, frowned: 'Not

217

at all. Kill the bastards, it ended the war.'

I got up and walked out, without a word. Bridget muttered something, I didn't hear what, and followed me onto the street. Where the sun glanced through the leaves of an old lime tree, and I felt ... I don't know ... cleansed, saved?

It's what we're up against. Bloomberg gives forty or fifty million dollars a year to the arts. Money buys influence, the validation of views like that.

No New York installation for me!

Let yourself have anything to do with them and, in effect, you endorse the system.

Lynn xx

P.S. Mother is out, gone, caput. Sorry, but it just doesn't feel right. You're Mum again.

—

Lynn
HAPPY BIRTHDAY
50 today
With lots of love
Mother

P.S. You're old enough to call me what you like!

[Mum wrote this on a very elaborate birthday card, groaning in plastic mini-fruits and glitter.]

29 JULY 15

Mum
Georgie and Gary took me out today for a birthday

breakfast at their favourite café, in Exmouth Market. It was lovely. Georgie has awful intestinal pains, worse recently than before, and is extra careful where and what she eats.

I like it when the three of us get together.

They live four months of the year in America, on their farm in upstate New York, the barns converted to separate studios. Georgie does the vegetable garden and Gary looks after the orchard, both of which they created from scrub. Don't have children. At least not together. Gary has a grown-up son, born when he was still a student at Goldsmiths and ... long story!

They've invited me over to stay whenever I want.

Maybe, maybe, one day.

For ages Georgie felt bad about living off Gary's money, her own work sidelined by the art trade. She accepts it now, trusting in the value of her contribution to his shows.

Her work is seen and sells more these days.

Gary is relaxed with money, never having had or expected any after leaving his Kent Estuary comprehensive at sixteen with only three O Levels. Until the YBA phenomenon erupted and made him rich. At breakfast he told a fun story about being interviewed recently and trying to make the journalist accept that, much though he admired Ellsworth Kelly curves and Brice Marden stripes, for example, the only paintings he cares about are his own. 'They're great artists,' he said, scoffing scrambled egg, 'I love their work. But what people don't understand is that the only person I'm really interested in is me!'

Yeah, Mum, don't say it! Me too!

It's true.

With love, Lynn

Dear Lynn

I understand Georgie. She's from Harrogate, I think she said. Where money counts. Does in Birmingham too.

Everyone judges you by what you earn. Admires the man who buys a round of drinks and, casual like, leaves the change on the bar.

Stands to reason it doesn't feel right to Georgie not to pay her share, in a good marriage.

I suppose Gary's a fancy cook too? Don't tell me!

At my age, L'Escala is pretty boring. Holiday spot for the young. Young-er, at least.

There're cafés on the beach where I like to sit in the shade, reading the British papers. Plenty in the supermarkets, half a day late. Occasional concert in the town hall. Nothing much else for the likes of me

The main trouble is my skin. Ten years on the Costa Brava and after ten minutes in the sun these days my skin erupts. Have to go about wrapped up to the gills, like an Arab.

I read a lot. Anything more to recommend?

Love

Mother

13 AUG 15

M

You're 'washed in the blood of the sun.'
That's Joyce!
L XXX

[This was on a postcard captioned *There were these thick paddies...*, designed by Bob Starrett, of a caricature cockney comedian telling a joke against Irishmen, the names of Beckett, O'Casey, Joyce, Wilde and Shaw emblazoned across the wall at his back.]

19 AUG 15

Mum

I've stopped trying to imagine what books you might like and simply list what I do!

Alphabetical by author this time, all novels published within the last five years:

Nadeem Aslam – *The Blind Man's Garden*.

John Darnielle – *Wolf in White Van*.

Viola di Grado – *70% Acrylic 30% Wool*.

Lars Iyer – *Dogma*. [I found this a bit too dense and philosophical, but noted a good quote: 'There is the reserve of the wise man, full of learning, full of modesty, who knows that the truth is infinitely subtle, infinitely complex, and that one must never speak too soon. And there is the roaring silence of the idiot, which resounds with dark matter and barren wastes and bacteria.']

Joyce Carol Oates – *Mudwoman*.

Emily Perkins – *The Forrests*.

Marilynne Robinson – *Lila*. [I was entranced, still am, by the first two lines of this novel: 'The child was just there on the stoop in the dark, hugging herself against the cold, all cried out and nearly sleeping. She couldn't holler anymore and they didn't hear her anyway, or they might and that would make things worse.']

Ali Smith – *How To Be Both*.

Christa Wolf – *City of Angels*.

Mostly women authors, as usual with me. Hope some of them fit your taste.

Did you hear what Aunt Betty gave me for my fiftieth? A Victoria Beckham handbag!

At least it was a fake, so not too ludicrously expensive.
Took it straight round to Oxfam on Kingsland Road.
When could she ever have seen me with a handbag in my whole life?
I suppose she thinks it's high time I grew up!
With love
Lynn

25 AUG 15

Mum
Probably becoming fifty makes me think – a little bit, not too much, really – about what the future might be for my work.
I mean, I don't care a bean about what happens when I'm dead ... when Richard and I are both dead. No, what bothers me is now, is how the work's seen now. How I am seen, in other words.
Stuffed with contradictions. Because art world reputation means nothing. None of that matters to me. Shit on status!
All the same, I would like better to understand public success, to work out why it has come to me while others also with visible talent never manage to get anything done publicly.
Then there are artists who do do plenty but no one takes a scrap of interest.
The genuine desire to create things that are meant to matter doesn't in itself equip anybody actually to achieve their aim, to persevere on and on in the working and reworking, the trying and rejecting, until something of meaning finally emerges.
You see, some sense!
Still a mystery.

Thoughts flap and scatter.
With love
Lynn XX

28 AUG 15

Mum
Sorry, I'm bad at answering your questions. I do notice, intend to respond, and then forget by the time I'm actually writing.
Better late than never, as you used to say, on picking me up from the library!
To let you know that both Georgie and Gary have made themselves into equally good cooks. From nowhere. No chef-stuff in either family. I remember once when I was round at their place mentioning that I loved the sound of apple tarte Tatin but didn't have a clue what it was. And next time we had dinner with them they'd made one. Together. Double delicious!
Same with growing things, they've taken to that too.
Georgie uses in some of her work the plants she tends in her garden in up-state New York, takes inspiration from the leaves and flowers. She's done a great series of photos of parts of her own naked body pressing up against luscious vegetables. Years ago, she made her bare bum into a car tax disc!
I'm less consistent in the sources I turn to, which helps explain, I suppose, why people find it a challenge to take openly to my films.
No harm, a little unease.
Love
Lynn

12 SEPT 15

Mum

I've been trying to assess how far I've got, what it is that matters to me. In a semi-philosophical sense.

Anyway, this is what I ended up writing, after several drafts.

There will never be an army of people marching to overturn the status quo, the idea a contradiction in itself. Armies wear uniform, function by repressive hierarchies of command. Armies shoot people. Feminists believe in freedom of expression, equality and governance by consensus. Outside the denizens of power, there are plenty of women in Britain who refuse to behave as the system requires of them, people who conduct their lives by different standards, who think and question and doubt. Some of them are writers, others are visual artists, creative individuals who these days make the essential difference to my life. I almost feel at home in the particular part of the world-of-art I have ended up inhabiting, shared mostly with forthright, creative women.

Something like that.

Nothing quite as clipped and tidy, perhaps.

No more to say at the moment. Just wanted you to see where I've got to, so far.

With love

Lynn xx

4 OCT 15

Mum

Was up in Cheshire mid last week. Nantwich. Visiting a man who's bought three of Richard's miniature paintings. I went unwillingly. Well, willingly in so far as Richard asked me to, wanted my support, but not wanting to go for myself.

In fact, it was fascinating. This man lives alone and hasn't much money, works for the County Council, in the housing department. And yet owns dozens of terrific works by contemporary British artists, all hanging in a patchwork across the walls of his modest flat, floor to ceiling.

In the kitchen, the loo. Bathroom, even.

It's amazing. Not just the works themselves, but his enthusiasm. And knowledge. And unpretentiousness.

Must be about sixty, short, with wiry grey hair.

Gradually, through the last fifteen years, he told us, he's found himself devoting more and more time to hunting down those things of high calibre which he can afford. Mostly drawings and prints, it's true. Of such interest and distinction, though.

He's arranged with his boss to take his weekends on a Wednesday and Thursday, working Saturdays and Sundays instead in the office. To give him the opportunity to visit art dealers and see exhibitions, in London and Manchester mostly. Viewing auctions when dates coincide.

Really heartening.

We spent the night in a guest house near where he lives, close to the town cricket ground.

He knows more about Richard's work than I do!

Love, Lynn

21 DEC 15

Mum

I've received this fantastic present: a Stone Cake!

Knowing that I throw away Christmas cards the moment they arrive, without opening them, and ban decorations, mince pies and turkey from the house, Lindsay has made me a marzipan fruit cake in the shape of a stone, with blue-grey smoky swirls brushed onto the white icing.

She's just as much an artist as I am. Shows how useless labels are.

If I had a smartphone I might have emailed you a photo! Shall I ask Richard to?

Lindsay once said, when I was feeling low, that I suffered from 'fragility of identity'. Then we talked through some of my films and she modified the suggestion, given how securely and independently I work, adding the adjective 'historical'!

Lindsay also pointed out that little I do satisfies me. Which hits the target.

Love

Lynn

3 JAN 16

M

You haven't done New Year for ages have you, since you stopped working in the pub?

I never do. Always work through public celebrations as if nothing has happened.

Still, I hope 2016 is good to you.

And here's a January quiz question: what does Lindsay do for a living?

Love, L xxx

[On one of Ann Rusnak's AIDS postcards from my collection, titled *Chastity Is Back In Style!*, which she published herself in Nevada in the late 1980s.]

L
She's probably something like a brain surgeon.
Maybe not, living on the Isle of Sheppey.
A weather forecaster?
Wait ... Something she said to me ... Is she a policewoman?
M xx

[An anti-Trump postcard designed by Jonathan
Horowitz and published in Brooklyn by Primary
Information, a photo of the back view of Donald Trump
on the golf course, titled *Does She Have A Good Body?*
No. Does She Have A Fat Ass? Absolutely, the sky behind
convulsed in a fire storm. I cannot imagine where, why
or how Mum acquired this brand-new postcard.]

18 JAN 16

Mum
Bull's-eye!
Lindsay is a Detective Inspector, no less.
Your barlady's empathy kicking in.
Seriously, it's why you were good at your job, by correct
assessing and natural sympathy. Kevin Southam told
me you were the best barman he'd ever employed.
Pity you took the cheer-them-up act too far and brought
them home with you!
Times long past.
Should it be 'passed'?
Either, maybe.
With love
Lynn X

Dear Lynn

The Blind Traveller was my home after you left. Everyone knew me.

Some pricks. Not too bad, by and large. There were blokes I slept with once or twice, who remained regulars in the pub. We became friends. Good friends.

It's different after you've had sex with someone. Even if you were both drunk.

My difficulties came with the unmarried ones, hard to get rid of. Too soft-hearted, that's my problem.

Like them, I also was lonely. It's me, how I've always been, for as long as I can remember.

Never mind. Used to it by now.

Love

Mother

7 APR 16

Mum

I spent yesterday afternoon with Bridget, at her gallery in Southwark, discussing an idea I have for a show of political art.

A group exhibition, one work by me, the rest commissioned from other well known artists genuinely committed to a particular cause. It'll take ages to organise, as we'll need to be careful who we choose. Artists are champion jumpers onto band wagons. Don't want that kind of careerist.

I told Bridget that, although I'd be happy to help behind the scenes, fronting the project is out of the question.

She suggested Patricia Bickers, the editor of *Art Monthly*, as curator. Which is an excellent idea. In her editorial only last month Bickers criticised large corporations with their tax haven assets, as well as the public institutions that increasingly depend upon them.

Bridget wondered if Mansfield Art was the right venue for an ambitious international show like this. I'm sure, I told her, that it is. We wouldn't want some gallery with acres of polished concrete floor. Her semi-domestic setting is perfect. And beautiful, I pointed out.

She'll talk to Patricia, whom she's known for years.

If you get the impression, Mum, that everything I think of gets done, you'd be very wrong! Those are just the ones I tell you about. I've had endless ideas which came to nothing, either because they were no good or because I couldn't get anybody in the art world to fly with them Same for my films. Sometimes I decide after months they're duds and wipe them from the record.

Ah well!

With love,

Lynn

P.S. Just so you know, Bridget has agreed to my ban against dealers exhibiting my films at art fairs. Instead she'll sell work direct, at moderate prices, to a few long-term friends, collectors and museums. In editions of no more than four, with a signed and counter-signed legal agreement that any resale can only be direct to me or to my heirs, at the original price plus a time-calibrated allowance for inflation. This massively reduces the financial value of my work. I couldn't care less. 'How much is enough?' To quote a Lawrence Weiner multiple. And he's worth listening to!

Mum

I wonder, in your experience, is there less prejudice against age than against race or gender?

Maybe there's no difference, repressive prejudice affecting all three equally.

Change, if it occurs at all, happens very slowly, apparent advances seen in retrospect to have been illusory.

Some improvements, all the same, even in my lifetime.

Many more female graduates; mass malaria treatment; genocide trials at the International Court of Justice in the Hague.

What have been the big changes you've seen? Been around twenty-five years longer than me!

Love

Lynn

—

Dear Lynn

Talk of age prejudice!

What about the fuss you made about my tattoo!

Told me I was too old for a tattoo, that it'd gone out of fashion, that I'm an embarrassment.

All because of a lovebird above my left tit.

What's it got to do with you?

Listen to yourself!

Sorry, love, it really annoyed me at the time. Got it off my chest now.

The biggest change in my lifetime has been Mrs Thatcher becoming Prime Minister. A strong woman. What the world needed, and admitted it.

Hope Theresa May doesn't get the job now. She'd let the female

side down, I guarantee. One of those women who never say
what they're really thinking.
Swings and roundabouts, same as always.
M xx

—

Dear Lynn
Could you send me ten packets of paracetamol?
I don't trust the Spanish pills and my headaches are killing me.
Not literally!
I'm fine, in general. Don't want you and Betty putting your
heads together to sort me out!
Mother xx

[Written on a postcard which Mum must have picked up at the café where she went for morning coffee, a supplier's promotional card for Mona de Pasqua, with a close-up photo of the top of one of their cakes.]

21 JULY 16

Mum
Annie, Fran's mum... Was once the other way round, Fran I used to describe as Annie's daughter and now she's the lead figure within my life. A touch unnerving. Fran's set to go travelling for a couple of years, in the Far East.
Anyway, Annie called by the other evening to tell me that her father had died suddenly, of a heart attack, on a fundraising cross-country bicycle ride in Cuba. She doesn't have to go out, as the charity is flying his body back.
I was surprised she didn't know what cause the charity

supported. Apparently, her father didn't much mind, it was the places which attracted him. This was the second big foreign ride he's done in six months.

Why on earth am I telling you this? First stage senility! Looks as though Fran takes after her grandfather, with her journeys abroad.

Hope your headaches are calming down.

Love

Lynn x

—

L

One advantage of drinking and smoking like a trooper all my life, I won't linger!

Last thing either of us need is me to be a gaga ninety-year-old. I'm not in the least bit afraid of dying.

M

P.S. My block of flats is off picture on the right.

[Mother wrote this on a tourist card of the harbour at L'Escala, with tall apartment buildings disappearing up the hillside.]

3 AUG 16

Mum

In case you think I'm the only maker who complains about the art world, Gary has left White Cube after they've represented him for twenty years. Gone to Monika Sprüth, a friend from early on. He's fed up with the ritual of art fairs and biannual solo shows.

Wants to make the work when he wants and show it when he's ready.

Not before.

Maybe not at all.

He's tough, Gary. Good on control. Always makes his own decisions.

Like me. It's one reason why we're friends.

Love

Lynn x

P.S. Just remembered you often saying, back then, that you were 'fed up to the back teeth' with me. You know I still can't really get a grip of this phrase. Find it pretty sinister, in fact.

22 AUG 16

Mum

My letters to you seem to me, in retrospect, annoyingly banal and art-gossipy, and I kick myself for posting a good few of them. Why didn't I take the time to write more thoughtfully?

Strange, because the result of writing to you is often to open up in my head quite complex thoughts.

And yet I send such stupid stuff to you!

After telling you earlier in the month a bit about Gary, I spent odd moments during the rest of that week thinking about perseverance. Which is a form of strength. A bloody-minded sort of self-belief. Necessary to becoming an artist potentially of merit.

Step by step in my thoughts I've ended up appreciating that the blinkered, disciplined life I lead, with few distractions from work, is the way things have to be. For me. And for Gary, for that matter, more or less. For quite a few makers, I suspect.

Anyway, that's what I reckon.

I'll try and remember this when the doubt-storms rage!
Love, Lynn xx

—

Dear Lynn

I've done something stupid. Not serious. Plenty annoying all the same.

Bought a smartphone online. Knew the moment I opened the package that the dinky little creature in its rainbow colours wasn't for me.

Don't know what made me get it.

Spooked me. Gave it away to Grania without even switching the thing on.

Honestly, I got to being afraid it'd spontaneously activate itself and take over my life!

Will stick to my old mobile.

Goes with the territory, old biddies losing their marbles. The other day I was trying to remember who's died this year. And couldn't.

Anyone gone I care about?

Don't miss Ronnie Corbett. Should have trimmed his silly eyebrows! Never had any time for Alan Rickman, another of those men with giant egos.

Did always have a soft spot for Bowie. Great looking. The make-up. Wow! What a pro!

Best foot forward.

Love, Mother x

18 OCT 16

Mum

I've become involved with an outfit called Contains Art, in Watchet, a tiny place on the Somerset coast near

234

Minehead. They're a tonic, putting on exhibitions and devising art projects for all the right reasons. They manage to do such wonderful things just in three marginally adapted steel shipping containers on the dock beside the old harbour.

Working with them calms me down, helps me see the sense again in making art.

I do what I can to help.

This includes a small show of my own which opened in one of the containers last week and was taken up strongly by the press. Difficult to resist WATCH IT headlines, perfect for lazy journalists! Never mind, got them noticed.

Contains Art really loves a party, and cooks free food for people attending private views. The Watchet pubs benefit from the after-flow. Not without incident. After the summer solstice party an older artist, sozzled, fell across the low brick wall outside his terraced house in the upper village and ruptured his spleen. The ambulance got him to Musgrove Park Hospital only just in time.

I was told all this. Didn't go myself. Three people for tea's my social limit!

I love going to Somerset, less than two hours on the train to Taunton, where an artist-friend, Bee, meets me. Puts me up for the nights I'm down in an annexe to her cottage on the hill. Backs onto an orchard with three pet rams, who bash the door with their heads when they notice I'm there, and wander into the guest kitchen! One is a Jacob, black and white with curled horns. Named Moses. What else?

In honour of my Israeli friend Lia I call him by the Hebrew, Moshe. Except we discovered the other day that Jacob sheep were first recorded three thousand years ago in the hills of Syria. So our Moses is probably a Muslim, and should rightly be addressed as Musa! He's a bit of a terror!

Charges, head down, at people he doesn't like and knocks them over!

Great sight rearing up on his hind legs to scrump apples. An old Somerset classic, Sops of Wine, is his favourite, juicy and sweet.

Love

Lynn

P.S. Last time I was down Bee told me something I hadn't heard before. That at his show in Wuppertal in 1963, the Korean sound artist Nam June Paik hung the freshly severed head of an ox above the entrance! 'Nothing new under the sun', you'd be able to say to that Damien Hirst!

17 NOV 16

More books, Mum?

OK

You could try Jenny Diski's *In Gratitude*. It's not a novel but a lot about writing and imagination. She's spiky, like you.

Diski died earlier this year, after publishing in the London Review of Books long and frank articles about her terminal cancer.

I loved *River* by Esther Kinsky. Set mostly in London, though.

Oh yes, there's Adam Thirlwell's *Lurid and Cute*. He'll sort you out! Maybe Ross Raisin and *God's Own Country*, set on a farm in Yorkshire?

That'll do you, for the time being.

My writer of the moment, in translation, is a German. Astonishing energy, and chutzpah. The things he dares to write! I'm keeping his name to myself for a while, a secret pleasure.

Let me know how you get on.

Lynn X

P.S. If I talk in detail about the books I like, they lose their power. Books feel most alive inside my head. All I would say is that I hope you one day have a go at Maggie Nelson. She's the sharpest, brightest writer imaginable. Her interests are not obviously yours, I know. You never know, though.

15 DEC 16

Mum

I was moved by something Georgie said to me the other day. We were trying to find the entrance to a newly opened gallery off Mare Street, where a friend of hers was exhibiting.

'The only secure place, for me, is an untouched sheet of drawing paper,' she said. 'I feel nothing is required of me by it. It's me in charge.'

I told her that I probably feel safest when I'm reading. Absorption in a brilliant novel protects me.

And there's the astonishment of feeling I've found a kindred spirit. The reassurance of discovering that such writers, such people exist.

For others, I know, reading is primarily entertainment. An escape from self, they say.

What about you? What does reading do for you?

Love

Lynn x

Dear Lynn

For me reading is reading. Begin at the first page and end at the last then pick up the next book.

I don't think as much as you do. People don't, we're too busy, earning a living, bringing up children. Down the pub.

Yes, it's true, for most people reading probably is an escape from the day-to-day. A way to relax.

Personally, I don't mind so much about that, and actually rather like reading books which I find so difficult to understand that enjoyment is hardly the word.

It's not about me, I don't think about myself, I get taken up with the writer, with what he or she seems to think. As far as I can tell from their book.

Do I pass? The right answer?
Love
Mother

5 JAN 17

Mum
With flying colours! Top of the class!
Love
Lynn xxx

[Another from my store-drawer of political postcards, this published by Recycled Images, titled *A Schoolgirl's Secret*, the drawing of three identical 1950s schoolgirls being ticked off by the headmistress, who says: 'In future my girl, you'll stick to domestic science.' The caption at the bottom of the postcard reads: *Doreen had been cloning herself in the labs again.*]

23 FEB 17

Mum
Susan has moved over to the Lisson Gallery.
I'm glad. They'll suit her better than Taylor.
Richard Long in their stable, the Sol LeWitt Estate,
Jonathan Monk, Laure Provost, Ai Weiwei, Ryan
Gander!
Now you know!
Lynn XX

[Wrote this on one of a stack of Jill Posener postcards
I have kept since I was a student, published by The
Women's Press. Posener travelled around the UK photo-
graphing feminist graffiti on posters. This is of a Pretty
Polly street billboard headlined WHERE WOULD
FASHION BE WITHOUT PINS?, the larger-than-life
photo of a pair of slim stockinged legs striding down the
catwalk, across the bottom of which is spray-written the
answer: *Free Of Little Pricks ... Stop Needling Us.*]

2 MAR 17

Mum
About my anti-rich phobia. Just wanted to say that I
realise there's nothing new about the pact between art
and money.
I mean, think of Joshua Reynolds.
Gainsborough too.
Don't know how you could have seen it, but there's this
stunning Gainsborough at Dulwich Picture Gallery.
Each visit I stand in front of it shaking my head in
amazement at the richness and vitality of detail, finding
it impossible still today to imagine how he dared invent

and then manage to execute these effects.

I've felt these same feelings about his picture of Elizabeth Moody and her young sons on every visit over the last thirty years, since I was at St Martin's. And on each occasion, I've also stamped and fumed at the excessive wealth of the people who paid for such massive portraits to be painted.

I know, I can hear you saying it: 'Don't make things so difficult for yourself. Life's too short.'

I disagree. In my view life is diminished by NOT trying to do something about these things.

With love

Lynn

—

Dear Lynn

Growing old's not great.

No two ways about it.

Things you'd never think about. Like my earlobes. Be brushing my shoulders in no time!

It's my own fault, I know. Wearing those big tarty earrings behind the bar all those years.

Looks worse now being so thin.

Must stop, need a fag.

Glad I never really gave up smoking. Annoys the hell out of you, but I can't help that.

Mother xxx

29 MAR 17

Don't apologise, Mum, I'm not annoyed. Not any longer. You must please yourself. Please do.

It's your right.

Much love, Lynn

[I remember searching through the drawer for a post-card Mum would really like, instead of just pleasing myself, and was happy to come across this 2001 postcard titled *Green Ray*, which an artist whose work I like a lot, Tacita Dean, made for Parkett: a still from the film she shot from the island of Murimbi, off Madagascar, hoping to capture the fabled moment when the sun setting on the horizon turns green.]

14 APR 17

Mum

I've been enjoying this wonderful period of uninter-rupted work in the studio. Which may explain why my recent letters to you have been so art-oriented. Have to admit that I spend little time thinking about anything else. No money worries to distract me. No relationship worries. No dealer worries.

Would you mind answering this: how confusing do you find my work in terms of fact and fiction?

Knowing as much as you do about me, I expect you must sometimes wonder which of the bits in my films that you don't recognise actually happened to me. More or less. And which are completely made up.

You haven't asked me, I know, but if you did, I'd rather not, even to you, give specific answers.

Can respond in general. Which is to say that I find it exciting how, in interweaving real and imagined events, the former often sound like the latter, and vice versa. What's more, I don't really believe that cold facts mean anything in themselves.

Didn't the reviewer of one of my shows write something of the sort?

Anyway, as you'll be more-than-aware by now, all my

work is personal.

It starts and ends with me.

My work is also an evasion, even a deceit. Because I describe only what it is possible to tell myself at the time, when the worst self-damaging thoughts and actions feel intolerable, beyond contemplation, and are therefore left unsaid, unsayable, even in the imagined form of a film. I hide things from myself, intentionally.

I'll stop. This is getting meaningless. My attempts at explanation always fail.

With my love

Lynn

28 APR 17

Mum

Richard's father has been to stay again.

I enjoy his visits. Normally only for a couple of nights. Though retired from the hospital, he still sits on a couple of advisory committees.

We took him to a documentary play at the Tricycle in Kilburn. Ate beforehand in their cafe. Enthusiastic service, lousy food.

Very good play. One of their series of political reconstructions, the best known probably the Saville Tribunal ten years ago. This one was an imagined dramatisation of the cabinet meeting at which Cameron secured agreement for a referendum on membership of the EU.

More dramatic on stage than it sounds, I promise!

They've become very skilful at the Tricycle in these reconstructions. Richard's dad loved it.

Lynn xx

Mum

Saul, the big ginger, has gone too. He'd been lying in an odd position behind a curtain. Although I felt him all over and found no point of tenderness at which he flinched, I took him to the vet in case.

Discovered he had raging cancer and should be put down. Poor Saul, I'd promised him, shut wailing in his basket in the taxi on the way the vet, that I'd bring him back home whatever happened. Richard was away, due back in four days, and I fed Saul titbits to keep him alive so the three of us could say goodbye together. The vet called to put Saul to sleep where he was, on our bed. Richard buried him beside Absalom, with heavy stones on top to stop badgers digging up the bodies.

I'm not sure life is possible for me without a cat.

Love

Lynn X

—

L

Sad about Saul.

He wasn't properly old, was he?

We had a budgerigar once, do you remember? Well, I had a budgie. You took not a blind bit of notice of it.

You were into battleships and four square and hangman, at the time. Paper and pencil games for two. Drove me to distraction! Dead against pets as a child, and now you're an addict.

Odd the way things turn out.

M xx

28 JUNE 17

Mum

You're right; although he was a bit fat, Saul wasn't old.
Not sure of his age as we inherited him. Captured him,
really. Asked neighbours if we could take him over.

Poor chap, slinking around the place, utterly unloved.
They were amazed anybody would want him.

Why, I wonder? What had happened for them to treat
him badly?

Such a lovely ginger puss.

We took ages, years calming him down. He used to flinch
at any sudden movement of the hand. Like a prisoner.

He was just coming into his own, six months ago for the
first time daring to sleep on our bed. I was so happy for
him. Saw him enjoying good years to make up for the
early loneliness. Then he went and died!

I'm sad. It seems so unfair.

Love

xLynnx

30 JUNE 17

Mum

I owe you an apology.

I used to be furious with you for lacking ambition. For
me and for yourself. The way you accepted prejudice.
Without complaint.

Now I'm aware what an advantage it's been to me that
you had few expectations, that I was free to take whatever direction I chose.

So, thank you. A bit late.

With love

Lynn

[Wrote this on a spare copy I had of Carla Cruz's post-card of the performance piece she titled *To be an Artist in Portugal is an Act of Faith*, for which she was photographed standing in her black bikini on an outside girder of the Ponte D. Luís in Porto, about to jump into the river below.]

—

Dear Lynn

You should've said something. You didn't ask so I didn't say.

It's not that I didn't care about unfairness it's just that I don't think things can change. People are shits. We're all shits. No two ways about it.

We're all, all of us, selfish and cruel and want our family to win at any cost. Want the nation to win, if you're that way inclined. Everyone likes to have an enemy to beat. Like football fans.

That's what I learnt as a teenager and seen nothing since to change my mind. The opposite. Everything's the same. More or less.

I'm glad to know you've felt free to choose, even though, personally, I don't really think anyone is.

Love

Mother

10 JULY 17

Mum

I'd no idea you thought such things.

Fatalism, you could call it. And yet you've always lived positively. I'd be in permanent depression if I thought like that!

Good for you.

I do agree that the majority of people are self-serving

and cynical, without an ounce of altruism in their brain. Can't hold back all improvements, though.

Think of what's happened during your lifetime to the position of women in society. Women as high court judges! Only achieved because a few people believed in the possibility of change.

Lots still to be done in education. Some of the social divisions, like sense of inferiority and fear around difference, would gradually dissipate if everyone went to school together. Look at New Zealand, Holland and Norway where fee-paying schools are virtually non-existent. Theirs are much less divisive societies than ours. Tub thumping. Apologies.

We'll see, we'll see.

Love

Lynn

P.S. You're probably right, nothing much really changes. Only the other day, I read about a sculptor called Charlotte Posenenske standing outside Documenta 4 in Kassel in 1968, where her work was exhibited, shouting: 'You culture vultures, so here you are all gathered together to chat and lie and talk crap so as to gain the upper hand.' In German. She spoke German. Because she was German! Fifty years later and I'm saying the same thing. In English. Because I'm English, unfortunately.

—

Dear Lynn

You remember that estate agent from Great Barr who was kidnapped, Stephanie Slater? You probably don't.

Anyway, she's died, of cancer, only fifty. In the Isle of Wight, where she moved to start a new life immediately after the court case.

She was adopted, apparently, the local paper says, or that's what
Charmian tells me.
Takes me back.
Can't avoid looking back, at my age.
With love
your Mother

P.S. Didn't I read once that Gillian Wearing, the one who won
the Turner Prize, comes from Great Barr? I must have some-
where that postcard you sent me. Didn't you rub out one of her
messages? Long time ago.

9 OCT 17

Dear Mum

A quiet Sunday at home. Time to digest the new feature
film that Ben Rivers has co-directed with a friend, pre-
viewed in the main BFI cinema last Thursday night,
evening two of the London Film Festival.

Have you met Ben? I've forgotten.

We've become friends over the last three or four years.
He and his girlfriend Yuki often come over for dinner.
Richard does the cooking, of course. Makes beautiful
Japanese food, with patience and precision.

Ben and I also meet up for tea at Leila's café on the
Boundary Estate, testing out ideas on each other. He
told me something fun the other day. That the Polish director Kristoff Kieślowski said about his films: 'After a
while I lose control of these incidents which I steal and
which I start to describe as having happened to me!'

Like me, Ben finds it hard to sleep, unable to switch off,
our minds racing with projects to film.

He did a Q&A after the festival screening, to a full house
of ... I don't know, five hundred people? Spoke of the

rewards of chance in film-making, the need always to remain open to unexpected, even unwanted occurrences. He told of coming across an old cinema and its caretaker late on in the shoot of *Krabi* and instantly knowing that he somehow had to make use of both.

Ben does these post-screening chats really well. Can't fathom how he manages to be so relaxed and natural. I'm the opposite. Get so nervous that I've stopped doing them. The curator, or Bridget, or someone else has to speak instead of me.

Can I tell you the plot? Because there is one, unusually for Ben! It's more or less covered here on the Information Sheet that they handed out.

You liked his *Ah, Liberty!* when I showed you a video at home on your August visit.

Are you putting some weight back on in the cooler weather? Hope so.

Love

Lynn

Krabi, 2562

Dir-Scr. Ben Rivers, Anocha Suwichakornpong

Cin. Leung Ming Kai

Sound. Ernst Karel

Prod. Maenum Chagasik

Cast. Siraphun Wattanajinda, Arak Amornsupasiri, Primrin Puarat, Oliver Laxe, Nuttawat Attasawat

UK-Thailand

2017

94min

This film combines the directorial talents of two notably different filmmakers who have, however, worked together before and create in *Krabi, 2562* a work of beguiling originality – Krabi, it should be noted, is a tourist town in Southern Thailand and 2562 is the current year in the Thai Buddhist calendar. Anocha Suwichakornpong, Ben Rivers' co-director, made her feature debut with the superb *Mundane History* (2009), concerning a paralyzed filmmaker and his nurse, along with his dreams and his movies (either in his head or to come, we can be never be certain). Her *By the Time It Gets Dark* (2016) drew a more political line in the sand, centring on the notorious 1970s massacre by police of students at Thammasat University, Bangkok. Suwichakornpong's narrative drive melds delightfully with Rivers' dreamier style, the latter coping with the film's all-Thai dialogue and crew and managing to maintain a central place for the rhythms and timbre of his film-sound through the design of research-focused experimental sonic artist Ernst Karel. The Thai cinematographer Ming Kai Leung is equally attuned to the Rivers aesthetic.

Outwardly a straightforward chronological narrative, there are enjoyable time-shifts in the second half, viewers almost believing that the missing young woman has reappeared – played by the only full-time actress in the cast, who is also alone in her occasional use of fluent English, her native Thai differently accented from the others. The cinema caretaker with his straggly half-beard is wonderfully himself, clear in the unscripted telling of his own actual story, with a crucial, unexplained date contradiction in his to-camera statement in the film, spreading a sense of unease about the fate of the girl, seen alive visiting alone the deserted cinema, fluid with bats. A locally celebrated Thai pop star plays the would-be-charismatic lead in a TV commercial being shot on the beach, his cool skewered by the black mop-head wig and subsequent appearance as a Neanderthal. Film-insider jokes include Rivers acting as camera-man for his director-friend Oliver Laxe's suitably indulgent portrayal of the ad-maker, and the scripting of the lead character as a location scout for an upcoming movie. Suwichakornpong's political bent is expressed in the unstated implication that these quietly beautiful landscapes will soon be lost forever in the contamination of rampant consumerism and invasive tourism.

Julian Williton. *Sight & Sound*, London

Krabi, 2562 opens with an investigation into a northern Thai location-scout's disappearance – the search for a searcher – then slip-slides into a tale of ancient cave-dwellers whose existence appears to happen both in the past and the present, and where young people work in the tourism and TV commercial businesses amidst the exotic glories of the vacation getaway spot of the southern Thai paradise of Krabi.

There are moving interludes, not necessarily essential to the basic story: in particular, the section with a retired travelling pugilist, which contributes significantly to the inner character of the film. The caretaker of an abandoned cinema undoubtedly plays himself and is simply brilliant on camera.

The cast is non-professional, largely playing themselves, much of the dialogue improvised, almost entirely in Thai. The dual directors, Ben Rivers and Anocha Suwichakornpong, together create an absorbing and playful portrait of a people, place and time that floats across fiction and reality, leaving haunting vignettes on the legacy of our age.

Chan Lai-kuen, *Hive Life*, Hong Kong

11 OCT 17

Mum

Do you know when you'll be over next?

Richard and I are dovetailing diaries, as one of us needs to be around to settle in our new kittens Dennis and Bert, tabby brothers from Cats Protection.

Let us know your dates, when you know them yourself.

Lindsay has been staying for several days, dealing with the aftermath of her stepsister's death, in a motor-scooter accident on the Walworth Road. She was riding pillion, I think. The stepsister, I mean.

The small spare room is always yours, whenever you feel like it.

I've again got myself fed up fit to burst with the barrel-loads of commercial money sloshing around the art world. Too few artists are aware how tainted they are by touching it. For years I've refused to exhibit at any of the Tates or the National Portrait Gallery, because of their BP connections.

Reputation-cleansing by the oil mercenaries, that's all it is. I'll have nothing to do with any of them.

Bought for Richard the other day an iron spice mill. Swedish. He says it's the best he's ever used. Shall I get you one too?

With love

Lynn

—

Sorry, love, but I don't feel like flying at the moment. Nor, actually, getting anything new for the flat. I'm hunkering down, keeping quiet and still.

Will be in touch when the planets shift. XXX

[Written by Mum on a piece of lined paper torn from a notebook and airmailed in a re-used envelope. Not sure why she did not email.]

4 NOV 17

Mum

I agree, take it easy for a bit.

Do they have bird baths in Spain? Must do, I imagine. You always loved yours in Sparkhill. I remember you closing your eyes and naming, by their shouts and songs, the birds lining up to compete for nuts.

Makes me think of an artist I've never met but whose work I've known for ages. He made ... oh, ten years ago now ... a wonderful piece on birdsong. Marcus Coates. He's with the same dealer as Ben.

His birdsong piece is a multi-screen installation showing ordinary people, of all ages, colour and gender, filmed in the bath, an underground car park, an osteopathic clinic, the bedroom, etc., adjusted by Coates so their mouths move to seem to sing the soundtrack songs of different birds.

Magical.

Dawn Chorus, he calls the series.

I recently saw his new exhibition. So funny. Got it into his head that formal apology was due by humankind for killing, in 1844, the last of the Great Auks!

So he made his way to Fogo Island, where this flightless bird used to live, and convened a committee of residents to decide, democratically, how the apology might best be phrased. He, of course, took the hilarious discussions dead seriously, recorded on video.

While visiting the Arctic, Coates found himself becoming fearfully conscious of the threat of climate change and set out to make another video, on Newfoundland, in which he imagined himself to be the last man alive on earth, standing naked behind ruined stone ramparts shouting into the void a list of man's inventions, in forlorn hope of justifying human existence. Delivered in hoarse desperation, melting icebergs floating by in the background, he struggled to think of unequivocal achievements, his words pursuing each other in an endless fifteen-minute video loop.

Good, eh?

I agree with Coates on the dangers of climate change. Don't you too?

We can all do something. I never use Amazon, for anything. Nor ever enter a Waitrose or Waterstones or Starbucks. The last two more because of how they short-change their staff than the air-miles.

Pretty feeble, I agree. I'll work on it.

Love

Lynn XX

13 NOV 17

Mum

The new little cats are hysterical.

They race noisily up and down the stairs. Then lie on the landing facing in opposite directions, paws forward, like the lions at Nelson's Column.

Bertie likes to play in my bath, banging around chasing his own tail. And rattling the metal chain on the plug!

Cats are the best!

Lynn xx

[Written on a new-at-the-time Lawrence Weiner postcard: the close-up of a woman's shoulder tattooed in black capital letters *Forever & A Day*, within his characteristic box borders with a red overlap, the same phrase tattooed on the artist's wrist, his arm embracing her.]

19 NOV 17

Mum
Must tell you.
I'm in New York. For work. Doesn't matter what.
And Gary has a show on at the Matthew Marks Gallery. It's called *MUM*. That's it, simply Mum, in big purple letters across the gallery window in West 22nd Street.
He told the New York Times that all his art is a valentine to his mother, Jill Henshaw.
I've met her, at a family dinner Gary gave at Eyre Brothers Restaurant, near the Hoxton Square branch of White Cube, where he was exhibiting at the time.
The absolute centre of her family of five children, whom she brought up alone, supporting them from her own modest earnings.
A librarian, I think. She glitters and glows.
She did until recently, when Alzheimer's took hold of her brain.
I like Gary. Like how openly he loves his mother.
I like the order and discipline of his studio. He insists, with a scowl: 'I'm a painter. Not an artist.' Been an RA since 2001!
Busy. Off now.
With love
Lynn x

—

Dear Lynn

You know my periods never stopped?

Too little oestrogen. Or maybe too much. I can never remember. It's not too bad. A bit sore, sometimes. Given up going to the doctor as I never understand what he says. Always used to think his English was quite good.

Perfectly normal, apparently. Though Betty'd never heard of it before. There's some ointment from the Farmacia which works OK.

Don't think it means I'll get pregnant!

Win some lose some.

Mother x

13 DEC 17

Mum

That's odd. Do you get normal period pains too, as well as bleeding?

That's hard luck.

No menopause symptoms, presumably? If you didn't, that'd be one plus.

I'm just about through. Wasn't too bad, luckily.

Sorry to hear you're in discomfort.

I'm not sure it's a good idea to stop going to the doctor, at your age.

Mightn't it be your hearing which has deteriorated, not his English?

When we saw you last summer, Richard and I had to speak much louder than we normally do. And you were always fiddling with your hearing aid, complaining that it wasn't working. Getting us to look if the battery had switched itself off.

There are brilliant new hearing aids these days. Microlight, simple to operate.

Would you take yourself to a specialist and order the correct type to suit your needs?

I'll very happily pay.

With love,

Lynn

P.S. I'm always adding PSs. Sloppy thinking! What I wanted to say is that I'm grateful for your strong character, determined to assume responsibility for yourself. I'll do, I trust, the same when my time comes.

13 JAN 18

Mum

Maybe it's me getting older, also the climate change statistics, but I've started feeling guilty about the amount of flying I do around the globe.

It's not necessary. Not if I develop ideas which can be filmed in Britain. Or Ireland, preferably.

Discussing these thoughts with Richard he admitted that his fear of flying all these years has been more to do with psychological than physical symptoms. That he feels sick in the head at the thought of flying, rather than in the stomach. He's horrified by the damage inflicted on the world by air travel.

Does his bit for climate change by wearing the same clothes for five days and cutting down on use of the washing machine. And powder.

Everything he owns is worn and washed with everything else!

We agree. On most things.

No car-owning as neither of us drive.

Our new rules. Stick to routine, get up at the same time, eat at the same time, go to bed at the same time. Keep

continuously busy. Face forward. Never waver!
What's more, I've discovered that I love English weather: rain, sun, sleet, mist, wind, thunder, snow ... all of it. The endless changes of the weather in a single day are wonderful, the clouds and sky shifting tone, the greens of grass and trees always different. Even in the mid-town park of Hackney Downs.
With love
Lynn

—

Dear Lynn
Richard's dead right about clothes.
Little girls with clean pants every day. Twice a day. Nonsense!
Whole families in flimsy clothes with the central heating blaring. It's not healthy.
Cheap rubbish. New! New! New! Latest! Latest! Latest!
Must matter too that it's mostly made in China? I don't get it. How these things come so far and are still so cheap.
Must be a better way of doing things.
Doesn't matter to me, I'm almost done now. Waiting at the exit. Good, though, that you and Richard make an effort.
Love, Mother

23 MAR 18

Mum
Not quite everything is dim and degraded in the art world: Helen Legg has been appointed Director of Tate Liverpool!
Ben and I both feel that Helen's the best curator of her generation. I'm surprised, though, that she's the Tate's cup of tea. Things are looking up!

AND she's from Birmingham. First at school, later working for Ikon.

Then ran Spike Island in Bristol, where she set up a non-hierarchical outfit. Gave me a solo show there in 2012. Beautifully installed. And, after the opening evening, instead of hurrying the artist and big-wigs off to some flash restaurant in the town centre, everyone sat together in Spike's own café for home-cooked kedgeree. With Helen now at the Tate I feel less isolated. Honest. Makes a real difference.

Much love

Lynn X

P.S. It's complicated. A big part of me wants my work to be owned by the Tate, one of the world's great collections of modern art. As it is already, both by Tate Britain and by Tate Modern. While the radical me detests their slimy crawl for money. Have you seen recently anywhere a current copy of Tate's quarterly magazine? At the hairdresser? On the back cover is an in-your-face colour photo of a leather handbag against white ground below LOEWE in large lettering. First double-spread at the front by Saint Laurent, followed by two Gucci pages, and then two Dior. Ultra glossy extravagance, nothing at all to do with contemporary art. Should be ashamed of themselves. Why not save the equivalent by reduction in size and say no thanks to tainted advertising money from the fashionista?

8 APR 18

Mum

One of the things I'd like to do one day is set up a small film club. To show work by alternative filmmakers. No particular genre: features, documentary, experimental. No conditions.

I'd want it to be for an audience of people like you, not just precious art-crowd-ees.

To precious add pretentious, pompous, pathetic, putrid, pitiful, phalse [ha!], permissive, parasitic, philandering, prosaic, puffed up. Plus plenty more.

It'd have to be in London, because that's where I am. More places have closed during my time than opened. Lux and La Scala have gone, though Close Up has started up and the newish Rich Mix is worth keeping an eye on. The ICA and BFI continue good programming.

I'll talk to Ben. He and three friends put on a six o'clock ICA screening once a month of work by independent filmmakers, which is well attended. They call themselves The Machine That Kills Bad People, after the Rossellini film!

Maybe Ben'd like to help me with something a bit more ambitious? We could perhaps persuade the Rio in Dalston to give us one whole evening a week. Mondays, say.

In dreaming of my ideal programmes I seriously do think, in my head, of you as the audience. I know you won't actually be there. You're ancient and live in Spain! And, it's true, I'd basically be aiming at a younger age group. It helps, though, to imagine how you might react to my choices. You never believe me when I tell you what good artistic judgement you have. Instinctively.

We'll see, we will see. My usual refrain.

With love

Lynn

P.S. Running an open-to-all film club would help show that art is for everyone who chooses to drop by, taking to it or not, as may be. People bring along whatever their experiences are, and that's fine, nothing more is needed. Will have to extract a slogan out of that, somehow. Billboard style!

13 APR 18

Mum

I hate speaking on the phone. Brings me out in a sweat. Another reason why I don't have a mobile.

Nobody uses the landline these days, happily.

You hardly ever do either. Except yesterday, suddenly.

It was really nice to hear your voice. You sounded ... not vulnerable, exactly ... softer than usual, less combative.

Don't worry about not writing, I'll assume you're OK until you tell me you're not.

Will continue to keep you up to date with what's happening to me.

With my love

Lynn x

8 MAY 18

Mum

To my surprise, cousin Gordon was in touch recently. We met up today, in the café at the ICA.

Was it late 2013 when we last saw him? At Aunt Betty's birthday. He's changed. Not for the better. And he was bad enough already then!

No, that's not fair. He and I've nothing in common, not his fault.

Poor chap, he's up against it. Sacked from his well paid job in Leeds selling insurance. Because of his gambling. Not with the clients' money, his own, leading to unmanageable debts. He's lost weight massively, and most of his hair. Messy clothes, clearly doesn't wash them or himself often enough.

Although he refrained from saying so, I know he wanted me to let him stay with us in Dalston. As he didn't directly ask, I didn't have to say no.

While we talked, I kept wondering what Gary would do. He's always been so generous, to his own family and Georgie's. Gary's wealthier than me. All the same, I'll ask his advice. Tomorrow, if he's in London.

Told Gordon that I'd have a think how I might best help. Promised to email within a couple of weeks.

I imagine Betty's bailed him out already as far as she can, without bankrupting herself too.

Love

Lynn XX

22 MAY 18

Mum

I'd been missing Lindsay and it was really good to meet up with her yesterday, at Victoria Station, in a juice bar. She'd flown in from Toronto at the end of a six-week international policing conference, and was catching the train home to Sheerness.

Apart from film-travel, I think of my life as pretty humdrum. Yet with Lindsay, my best friend, far away for a couple of months, I see that loads of things happened that I needed to talk to her about.

Anyway, she's back now.

Smart woman, been promoted again.

Loaded down with Canadian gifts for family and friends. Nothing for me, thank goodness, aware of my aversion to presents. Receiving or giving.

She was interesting on the topic of Gordon. In her professional experience of those criminals who are also addicts, alcoholics, gamblers and the like, the temptation to lie and manipulate in order to placate the urge is close to pathological, she says. And the best way to help is often not to. Not to help, that is. Not directly, not taking over. Helping them to find a long-term solution to the problem themselves.

Gary said much the same, in a completely different way. Market day. Promised Richard to buy some fresh bamboo shoots, daikon radish, and horenso spinach. Better get a move on. Not dressed yet!

Love

Lynn xx

19 JULY 18

Mum

You must fly over soon, to see the cats! They're terrific! Dennis and Bert are rivals for our affection, Bert worse than Dennis. When I'm alone Bertie instantly jumps on my knee and spits at Dennis if he comes anywhere near. Richard's arrival drives him mad, as he belts back and forward between the two of us, in a vain attempt to occupy both laps at once!

I wonder how old they are? Cats Protection said they thought they were about eight months old when we got them. Difficult to be sure as they're both small, and thin. Near-identical tabby twins. About a year and a half by now, I reckon.

I love their fastidiousness. Stretching out back paws to lick and spit in between their toes!

Richard is very good with cats, his movements calm. And quiet voice.

My husband of eleven years. How extraordinary.
You and I, Mum, we're loud mouths!
With love
Lynn x

25 JULY 18

Mum

For a non-people person, as you agree that I am, I actually have half a dozen or so really close friends. With whom I'm in frequent contact.

Jamie dropped by this evening, for example. A few years ago he invented, as an artwork, an experimental rock band called Lustfaust, mapping out performance schedules, writing songs, creating a website, even naming a fan base and faking their social networking.

He called in for a coffee on his way to work, three-nights-a-week driving a van around North London trying to rescue rough sleepers. Drug addicts mostly, and alcoholics. Both, as often as not. It's a battle, Jamie says, to persuade anyone to come with him. They prefer an independent life on the streets, however precarious, to external control in a hostel. He spends half the night sitting beside them in doorways, chatting, keeping them company.

I like Jamie. His Mum makes and remakes enormous jigsaw puzzles on a table by the back window of her home in Leicester.

I've elected myself chair of the Makers Brought Up By Mothers Club. The by-me-appointed members so far are Gary, Gillian, Jamie, Duncan, Katrina, Carl, Andy, Jonathan, Ruth, Jess, Ray, Ahmed, Ben, Georgie and Rebecca. I'm not sure Jess quite qualifies, as she's a magazine editor. And wasn't there a dad about the place, some of the time?

All the same, if I'm going to be in a club, Jess has got to be a member too. We've been friends since junior school. Do you remember when, for months, we pretended Sparkhill was called Eureka Springs? It was Jess who came across the name, on a map of Arkansas.

Bye for now.

With my love

Lynn X

8 AUG 2018

I was NOT here.

x

[In New York, arranging a screening of my recent work at White Columns, I found in a second hand book-shop this large pre-attack postcard of the Twin Towers. Marked a large X in black biro by a window of the 95th floor and wrote on the back: I was NOT here. Posted the card to Mum in Spain.]